GRACIE LINDSAY

BY THE SAME AUTHOR:

HATTER'S CASTLE

THREE LOVES

GRAND CANARY

THE STARS LOOK DOWN

THE CITADEL

THE KEYS OF THE KINGDOM

SHANNON'S WAY

THE GREEN YEARS

THE SPANISH GARDENER

BEYOND THIS PLACE

CRUSADER'S TOMB

THE NORTHERN LIGHT

THE JUDAS TREE

A SONG OF SIXPENCE

A POCKETFUL OF RYE

THE MINSTREL BOY

LADY WITH CARNATIONS

Autobiography:

ADVENTURES IN TWO WORLDS

GRACIE LINDSAY

by

A. J. CRONIN

LONDON
VICTOR GOLLANCZ LTD
1978

First published in serial form in 1949

ISBN 0 575 02412 7

MADE AND PRINTED IN GREAT BRITAIN BY
THE GARDEN CITY PRESS LIMITED
LETCHWORTH, HERTFORDSHIRE
SG6 1JS

Chapter I

IT WAS ON the fifth of May in the year 1911 that Daniel Nimmo got the news of Gracie Lindsay's return. All that afternoon, which was warm and full of the promise of a fine summer, he had been pottering in and out of the dark-room of his little photographic studio preparing for an appointment with Mrs Waldie and her daughter Isabel.

At three o'clock they had not arrived. He sheathed his silver watch with the yellow horn guard, and gazed mildly through the flaking whitewash on his window into the empty street.

Dressed in an old cutaway coat, too tight and short for him, shiny black trousers, a celluloid dicky and a stringy black tie, Daniel was a shabby, an insignificant figure. His cuffs were of celluloid also, to save the washing, and his boots might have done with mending.

His expression was thoughtful, absent, timid, and his lips, surprisingly rosy, were pursed, as if he were about to whistle. Not that Daniel would have whistled—he was too scared of drawing notice to himself. He was, indeed, a quiet, humble little man who had lived his 54 years without once creating the impression of importance.

The ra-ta-tap of hammers from the nearby shipyard made the air drowsy. They were building a new steamer for the Khedive Line—a fine order brought by the new agent, Mr Harmon, that would set trade buzzing in the little burgh of Levenford. By turning his head Daniel could see the big yard gates, dark green in the dull grey wall, opposite to Apothecary Hay's premises on the corner.

Even as he looked a four-wheeler swung around Hay's corner and came rolling and bouncing over the cobblestones towards him. A moment's pause, and two women, edging their wide hats and leg-of-mutton sleeves fastidiously from the recesses of the cab, advanced across the pavement. The bell rang and Daniel, clearing his throat, hoping that the stammer which was his habitual affliction would not trouble him, turned to receive them.

Mrs Waldie, the contractor's wife, entered first, her stout, comfortable form inclined a little forward, a long, rolled umbrella cradled in her arm and whalebone supports in her high net collar. Behind came Isabel.

Daniel, never quite at ease, had hurried forward with an offer of chairs and an observation about the weather, and now he took refuge in manoeuvring the camera while Mrs Waldie, glad to sit down in her tight button boots, watched him amiably, her red face shining with maternal fondness.

"We want a good likeness, Mr Nimmo," she said indulgently, with a glance towards the faded chenille curtains screening the alcove where Isabel had gone to remove her hat. "You understand the circumstances?"

"Indeed I do," Daniel answered. "And very happy ones too."

Elizabeth Waldie smiled. She was a good-natured woman, despite her over-dressing and the pretence of style that her husband's position demanded of her.

"We are pleased about the engagement," she went on. "Mr Murray is such a promising young man."

"Yes," Daniel agreed. "I've known Davie since he was a boy. A fine, steady fellow. And a good lawyer, too."

Here Isabel came from behind the screen, a faint, conscious flush on her cheeks. She was a fresh-complexioned girl, brown-haired and blue-eyed, and of a plump, somewhat heavy figure.

Although pretty enough in her way, her general expression was dull and rather spoiled—her lips in particular had a petulant droop. However, she looked pleasant enough just now, at this state visit to the photographer's, as though gratified that her likeness would soon be in a silver frame among the law papers on the desk of David Murray's High Street office.

"Mother thought that I should have a background of a balcony."

"It's very fashionable," Daniel nodded. "And, perhaps, with a book."

"Yes," said Mrs Waldie. "As though reading."

Again Daniel inclined his head and, lowering the dusty roller back-screen of a marble balustrade, he posed his subject with an open volume beside a bamboo plant stand. His grey eyes were earnest behind his steel-rimmed spectacles, his little brown beard cocked at an angle both ludicrous and touching, as he strove for artistic satisfaction.

"You might droop the left wrist a little more, Miss Isabel," he suggested finally, contemplating the effect with his head tilted to one side. Then he disappeared beneath the black cloth of the camera and exposed a series of mahogany-bound plates.

The operation over, Isabel resumed her hat and Daniel escorted the ladies to the waiting cab where, in parting, Mrs Waldie genially remarked:

"We'll expect you at the wedding next year. I'll see you have an invitation."

As he turned back into the studio Daniel was grateful for that show of kindness, for he well knew that, measured by the yard-stick of Levenford opinion, he was regarded as a failure—a ridiculous, incompetent failure.

The truth was that, nearly 30 years before, Daniel became a minister of God, duly licensed in the cure of souls according to the Church of Scotland. Yet Daniel had never found a pulpit.

At the outset his prospects had been good, there was interest in the young man who had taken all these prizes at college. With true native reverence for "the book-learning", Levenford proposed him for the parish church assistantship and named him to preach a trial sermon.

Daniel had such a sermon in his head, a fervent and well-reasoned sermon; for weeks past he had rehearsed it walking the countryside around Levenford with rapt eyes and moving lips. As he ascended the pulpit he felt

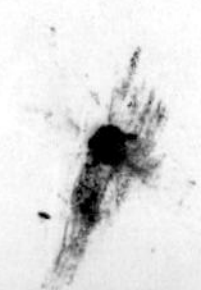

himself word-perfect. He announced his text and began to speak.

For a few moments he went well enough, then all at once he became conscious of his congregation, of those rows of upturned faces, those eyes directed towards him. A shiver of self distrust swept over him, the more agonising, more paralysing in its effect since he knew the dreadful sensation of old. The blood rushed into his face, his forehead, his neck. He hesitated, then halted, lost the thread of his ideas, and began to stammer. Once that frightful impotence of speech had gripped him he was lost. He laboured on, of course, pale now and trembling with heavy beads of sweat breaking on his brow, the lyric ardour of his discourse turned to something pitiful. With every shrinking pulse of his soul he sensed and magnified the reaction of his listeners to his own deficiencies.

While he toiled and struggled for the words he saw the restlessness, the ripple which followed the realisation of his distress, the side glances, the half-hidden smiles. He saw the children nudge each other; he even heard, or fancied that he heard, a faint titter, hardly suppressed, from the shadow of the gallery, where the farm servants had their seats. At this he broke down completely.

Never did Daniel live down that first debacle. He tried and tried again, going as far as Garvie in the North and Linton in the East in his attempt to find a church, yet always without success.

Twice he managed to reach the "short leet" in small country parishes, but, when it came to the ballot, in neither case was he "voted". Gradually he came to accept the mantle of the "stickit minister" and, obliged to find some means of livelihood—in the early upsurge of his hopes he had married—he fell back upon the skill which he possessed with the camera, becoming accepted in time as the town's official photographer.

Here the steeple clock struck five, and Daniel locked up the studio for the day. Then, according to his custom, before setting out for his home on the northern outskirts of the town he crossed the street to have a word with his neighbour, Apothecary Hay.

The druggist's shop was dark and narrow, and musty with the smell of aloes, asafoetida and liquorice root. Shelves of dark green bottles filled one side, and behind the long counter, close to a gas jet that stuck out like a yellow tongue on a marble slab spattered with red sealing wax, stood the druggist himself, compounding a pill with acrimonious melancholy.

Apothecary Hay was a lean, cadaverous man with a long bald head streaked with ginger hair, and drooping whiskers of the same colour. He wore a short alpaca jacket, green with age and the stains of drugs, which showed his bony wrists and his death's-door shoulder blades. His air was sad and bilious, his attitude that of the most disillusioned man in the whole universe. Nothing surprised him. Nothing, nothing!

And he believed in nothing—except strychnine and castor oil, John Stuart Mill and Charles Bradlaugh. He was Levenford's professed free-thinker. He cared for no one, not even his customers. He threw his pills and potions across the counter as though they were rat poison. "Take it or leave it," he seemed to snarl. "Ye've got to die in any case."

He seemed, indeed, to take a singular delight in the shortcomings of humanity—that was his sense of humour—and yet in some strange fashion, perhaps the attraction of opposites, he was Daniel Nimmo's closest friend.

Two other men were in the shop which served as the district's unofficial club—David Murray and Frank Harmon, the Khedive Company agent, and it seemed to Daniel that as he entered a sudden silence fell.

Harmon, a newcomer to the town, was a bachelor of forty, a tall, finely set-up figure in well-cut, cosmopolitan clothes, with thick curly hair, strong white teeth, and an air of restless vitality beneath the careless expression upon his florid face.

He nodded easily towards Daniel, and reached for the "pick-me-up" on the counter before him. Murray, on the other hand, was noticeably subdued, disinclined to meet Daniel's eye. A good-looking young fellow of 27, pale, dark, with cleanly chiselled features and hair which needed cutting falling untidily across his brow, he kept tugging at his short moustache with a sort of strained intensity.

"Good evening, all," said Daniel pleasantly. "I hope you're well, Apothecary."

Hay took no notice whatsoever of this remark, but went on grinding with his pestle, pausing only to bite off a sliver of liquorice root which he took from the side pocket of his faded jacket.

He was inordinately fond of the root, and he chewed

it continually with a peculiar acrid rinsing motion of the jaws, as though trying, pertinaciously, to gnaw a hole in his own cheek. This continued for some minutes, but at length, without raising his head, he spoke from the corner of his mouth.

"You haven't heard the news?"

"No," Daniel smiled. "Is the town on fire?"

"It may soon be!" There was a pause, then giving the words their full emphasis, Hay declared: "Your niece . . . Gracie Lindsay . . . is coming back to Levenford."

Daniel remained perfectly still. At first he did not seem to understand the other's meaning, but gradually his face changed. Reading his emotion, Hay went on with a dry constriction of his lips.

"It would appear her husband died—up-country in Mysore. Gracie sailed last week on the *Empress of India*."

Still Daniel said nothing: he could not speak, all sorts of instincts were rushing upon him. He turned mutely to Harmon, from whom he knew the information must have come.

"Yes," the agent explained, with good-natured condescension, "we had word from our Calcutta office this noon. Nisbet Vallance contracted blackwater fever while surveying a new railroad for the company. His wife was with him. Behaved very pluckily, I believe, getting him out of the hills by stretcher. A charming woman. I met her last time I was in the East."

Daniel swallowed the lump in his throat.

"Forgive me, gentlemen." He blinked apologetically

from one to the other. "This is a great surprise . . . after seven years . . . so unexpected. . . ."

"Quite a shock for you." Hay spoke with that same peculiar inflexion.

"Yes," said Daniel simply. "Poor Nisbet. . . . But it is a joy to think of having Gracie with us again." He turned warmly, almost appealingly, to Murray. "She was a sweet lass, was she not, Davie?"

"Yes," Murray muttered, without looking up.

There was a longer silence. Daniel unfolded his handkerchief and wiped his brow and neck.

"It's been close today. Very seasonable weather. Now, if you'll excuse me, I'll go home. I must see my wife. I dare say she's had word. Good-night, gentlemen."

He went to the door, opened it, and closed it quietly behind him.

So it was true, then, at last, what he had not dared to hope for all these years. As Daniel started on his walk home, by the quiet back road leading across the common, a wave of sweetness swept over him and his mind was filled by the tender vision of Gracie, his dear niece in her white dress—she had always loved white, and looked so beautiful in it—as he had last met her, one evening just before the tragedy, walking along Levenside with a bunch of meadowsweet in her hand. She had picked the flowers from the green river bank.

What a picture she made! The sun striking low upon the water set a radiance about her—"As a young roe come unto the river to drink"—instinctively the words had risen to his mind. Her face, vivid and small, was alive with animation, her warm brown eyes sparkling with the promise of life.

But what had she known of life at 18 years, poor child? He sighed deeply and his expression turned sad. But it brightened again as his thoughts travelled farther back and other, happier images crowded in upon him.

Among these, he saw her at the Children's Cantata given under his direction in the old Burgh Hall. What a wonder she had been, what a little wonder—only ten years old, with a voice like a flute, such liveliness and grace and talent—well, never, never had he met talent like it since.

He smiled—for now he watched her at the Academy prizegiving, coming up for the calf-bound *Pilgrim's Progress* she had won for Scripture knowledge—yes, he had coached her to win that, the best pupil he had ever had in his Bible class!

And again he saw her at the school picnic, a little thing of 12, a nice new ribbon in her hair, running in the small girls' race, her thin legs twinkling, her pointed chin set forward in a passion of endeavour, and winning as he held the tape, yes, winning to his great delight.

Daniel's eyes were misty now—he had cared so much for Gracie, with all the affection of a childless man. Somehow she was different from the common clay, finer, more precious in body and soul.

And somehow it had always seemed as though her father, Tom Lindsay, widowed when his only daughter was born, had never understood or appreciated her. Tom, at one time a thriving merchant in Levenford dealing in grain, fruits and provisions, and in his heyday Provost of the burgh, had a harsh and irascible temper, and, towards the end, the business worries which culminated in his bankruptcy had hardened and embittered him.

Of course there were those who whispered that his actions towards Gracie were justified, but this Daniel never would concede, and with a sharp, indrawn breath, he once again reviewed the calamity which had so broken up her life.

It was the winter of 1903, and Gracie at 18, with her hair up and skirts down to her ankles, was like a rose just coming into flower, the belle of all the dances, waltzing her way into every heart.

Slim and sweet and gay, with some secret sparkling quality, she had no lack of beaux. What a Christmas that had been! When the hard frost came she skated on the Pond, hands in her tiny squirrel muff, her cheeks whipped by the wind, while the young men of Levenford flashed around her, cutting the figure eight, doing the outside edge, showing off, trying to attract her notice.

"Gracie's a great one for the boys!" people had smilingly remarked. "They buzz about her like bees round a honey jar." Well, that was true enough. There was young Simpson, the doctor's son, Jack Hargreaves, and a score of others, yet most favoured of all was David Murray, then studying law at the University of Winton.

It was generally believed that David would be

Gracie's choice, when Henry Woodburn came upon the scene visiting his cousins, the Ralstons, who owned the shipyard in the town.

He was a stranger to the district, this Woodburn, a fair-haired fellow with a cough and slightly hollow cheeks. He drove his own dog-cart, a handsome turn-out, and had ample money and leisure.

Gracie had gone driving with him often in the evening, warmly wrapped in thick rugs when the soft haloed moon climbed above the hills of Garshake and the racing tattoo of the horse's shoes rose crisply from the frosted road.

There was some talk, of course, rumours that Woodburn was a wild young man who drank more than he should, that his lungs were affected, and that he really had been sent to this northern climate to recover his health.

But when reasoned with mildly, Gracie merely laughed in her droll and captivating way. She had always mocked the proprieties and never had her mood been gayer, more teasing or more utterly bewitching than on that evening by the river when, kissing Daniel lightly on the forehead, she had darted off to keep an appointment with Henry.

That same night, spanking home late from a visit to Loch Lomond, the horse shied at a shadow. Woodburn lost control of the animal, and at a turn of the road the dog-cart careened into a ditch, smashing violently against a stone wall. By some miracle Gracie remained unhurt. Henry was killed instantly.

For some weeks Gracie remained indoors, then with

her father she departed somewhat abruptly for Edinburgh. This seemed natural enough—she had need, surely, of rest and change—yet a feeling of surprise deepened in the town when several months went by and still Gracie did not return.

Then events took an even stranger turn as news came back that Gracie had married Nisbet Vallance, a civil engineer of 35, a steady, plodding sort of man, of no particular family or personal distinction, who had been on leave from his post as supervisor of the Central India Railroad to take a technical course at the Levenford shipyard.

No one had ever suspected that Nisbet, while regarded as a decent fellow, would ever aspire to Gracie. Yet married they were, in London, and left immediately from Tilbury for far-off India. And when Tom Lindsay returned to Levenford, even then beset by the business troubles which were increasingly to torment him, his grim, forbidding face deterred even the most presumptuous questioners.

Nevertheless, in a town such as Levenford the matter could not long remain a mystery. At least, the truth was rumoured and suspected.

It had all weighed heavily on Daniel. But now, walking with a rapt and fervent face under the faint twilight stars, he saw at last the chance to right an infamous and long-enduring wrong. At that moment the hand of Providence had never seemed more real to him. And in his breast, fanned by a rising exaltation, there was kindled the fire of a great endeavour.

He reached his house, a small red sandstone villa

at the end of the toll road, and stood for a minute in his tiny, perfect garden, one of his few earthly vanities, where around the trim lawn the neat beds of primulas, snapdragon and calceolarias had already begun to bloom.

He breathed deeply once or twice, then, wiping his shoes carefully—Kate, his wife, forbade the slightest mark upon her spotless linoleum, and indeed in winter she made him remove his boots before entering—he went in. His heart was beating faster than usual, with a sense of expectancy and suspense.

Yes, it was there, on the table, where his tea, as usual, was set out, a rice-paper letter with an Indian postmark, and Kate had opened it. Inquiringly he gazed towards his wife as she stood, in troubled fashion, pushing back a lock of her iron-grey hair.

She was a grey woman, four years Daniel's senior, and prematurely faded to neutral tints of unfruitful middle age. Her brow was good, even generous, despite the furrow which disappointments and frustrations had planted between her eyes, but the lower part of her face, the thin nostrils and the indrawn mouth, had been shaped by weariness and secret strife.

Her dress, cut from a "remnant" and made by herself on the treadle sewing machine that now stood, shrouded, by the window, was of homespun, old and drably grey, held together, or so it seemed, by the enormous cairngorm brooch planted in the centre of Kate's bosom. This brooch, which opened behind, disclosing a plaited relic of her grandmother's hair, was a solemn family heirloom and, save for her wedding ring,

Kate's sole article of jewellery. Somehow it seemed to emphasise the pathetic flatness of the barren bosom on which it rested.

"Kate," Daniel said at last, "she is coming back?"

Slowly she nodded.

"We'll have her here?" He spoke quickly, as though fearful of her decision.

"Yes, Daniel, we must have her here. And she'll be welcome too." Kate hesitated, then in a low tone added: "But, oh, I hope . . . in these years . . . she has learned to behave."

Soberly she came forward and began to pour his tea.

Chapter II

IT WAS SATURDAY, a brisk, fresh day, with sunshine in the air and woolly puffs of cloud tumbling gaily across the blue sky. You could see a long way off. From the toll road it was possible to make out the sheep, moving high upon the Winton hills, and to the west, where a little tug-boat stood far out on the choppy water of the firth, you could clearly read the number on her bright vermilion funnel. A lovely day for Gracie's homecoming!

Daniel and Kate were at the station early, 20 minutes before the ten o'clock train was due. Kate wore her new black dress and Daniel his Sunday suit. Turning the whole thing over in his mind as they marched in silence along Station Road Daniel told himself, with a full heart, that Kate had been splendid in all the arrangements she had made. The spare bed-room, an airy, pleasant room facing to the front, was now actually referred to as Gracie's room, and Kate's preparations there had been heroic. Muslin curtains had been hung, the furniture shifted to fresh positions, a new bedside rug laid upon the floor.

It was an agitating wait, but at last came a whistle and a flying pennant of steam, and the train pounded round the bend into the station. Doors flung open, a few everyday people stepped out, yawning and folding newspapers, and then, quite suddenly and simply, Gracie herself was on the platform, so real, so undeniably home at last, that Daniel's heart stood still.

For a moment she remained poised, vividly outlined against the drab background of the train, her gaze going hither and thither uncertainly, expectantly. All at once she saw them. Her eyes lit up, and with a little cry of rapture she ran forward, both her hands outstretched, too overcome even to attempt to speak.

She kissed Kate's cheek, then Daniel's, light as the touch of a bird's wing. She was so little changed the shock of it was startling. Daniel felt his eyes grow dim. Perhaps she was more fragile than before. Yet she had always had the quality—and now her mourning black intensified it.

Behind her little spotted veil her small, pale face was still alive and bright, and she had the same trick of pointing her chin, as if in animated inquiry of life. Her thick brown hair had the same quick reddish lights in it. Her eyes, of the unforgettable red-brown tinge, could still smile beneath their tears.

She was now both laughing and crying, on her way to the cab which Daniel, pale and flustered, had summoned from the station archway. Mastering his feelings, for he felt the seasoned eye of the jarvey fastened curiously upon him, Daniel saw the luggage stowed, while Kate and Gracie stepped inside. A moment later he joined them, and they were off.

As they bowled along Gracie impulsively yielded a hand to each of them, sitting a little forward, her gaze fixed through the open window, tender and entranced.

Each familiar object drew from her parted lips the same sound of recognition—the Burgh Hall, the Library, the grey stone front of the Academy, yes, even Luckie Logan's low-browed candy shop where as a child she had bought her "sweeties", all had their part in the ecstasy of her return.

There was nothing beautiful, God knows, in the architecture of these buildings—they were small and weather-stained, beneath the cold slate roofs, to a bleak and dreary grey—yet for Gracie they had a rare appeal, the warm salutation of dear, familiar friends. The absence of change particularly excited her. The smell of hot rolls drifting out from Carrick's bakehouse sent a tiny shiver through her body.

"It's all the same as ever," she kept whispering in between. "And, oh, it's so good to be back."

Gracie was always like that: acutely sensitive to the most delicate impression. A blink of sunlight on the muddy water of the common pond would make her stand catching her breath; a whiff of autumn wood smoke from Garshake would set her dreaming all the afternoon. And now an emotion, more poignant and more personal, the supreme emotion of her return, was catching at her throat with suffocating intensity.

As they turned down Church Street and came to David Murray's office she gave a little gasp and pressed Daniel's hand.

"Look! Look! I believe I see Davie at the window. Oh, Aunt Kate, can I stop and have a word with Davie? It's like a hundred years since I last caught sight of him."

Kate's expression was a study. Murray's clear-cut, shadowed features were indeed visible, as he watched, almost covertly, it seemed, from behind the curtained window.

"I don't think we'll stop just now, dear. You must be tired after your long journey."

"But I'm not the least tired," Gracie replied, with eager eyes.

Kate managed a smile, solicitous and controlled.

"There's so many people about, my dear. You wouldn't want them to see you running into David Murray's office the minute you were home."

Gracie opened her lips to protest, then closed them. Perhaps Aunt Kate was right. She must not be impatient. With a sigh she relaxed and sat back, conscious, though uncaring, of the fact that curious eyes were watching the passage of the cab through the town, that heads turned, tongues wagged, and nods were interchanged.

James Stott, butcher and acting Provost of the burgh, swathed in his blue-and-white apron and suitably hung with steel, was hooking a half-bullock at the door of his establishment and passing the time of day with Apothecary Hay. At the sight of the cab Hay rubbed his hands together till the knuckles cracked.

"Well," he said, dryly, "there she goes, Provost."

Stott took up the druggist's ironic tone. "It's a handsome equipage," he remarked, with a satiric eye on the dilapidated four-wheeler. "I suppose you would call it a return in state."

And the Reverend Douglas Mowat, minister of

the parish, walking down Church Street with his wife, while avoiding all comment, infused his portly person with an air of righteous reproach.

At last, however, the cab reached the toll road, and Gracie entered Daniel's house, enwrapped by a sweet haze. Those seven years in India had in many ways been hard for her to bear, yet now she was here they became obliterated, almost as if they had never been at all. Levenford was her home: she had never wished to leave it.

After lunch, at which she ate but little, she produced her presents, a fine Kashmir shawl for Kate, and for Daniel a set of brushes with carved ivory from Cawnpore. Then taking Daniel's arm, she drew him to the little garden and they began to pace the lawn. A note of charming earnestness mingled with her vivacity and misted her lovely eyes as she said impulsively:

"Dear Uncle Dan, your welcome means so much to me. It gives me new hope and confidence." There was a pause, then, sensing his silent sympathy from the touch of his fingers on her sleeve, she continued with an intimate smile: "I am not well off, you know—not one of those rich widows one reads of. Oh, I daresay I shall have a pension from the company but only a small one. I may have to earn my living: and I want so much to do something useful. You don't know how wasted these last years have been. I'm not blaming Nisbet: he was decent to me, poor man. But I never really belonged out there. This is where I belong, Uncle Dan, and now that I'm back I want to make a real future for myself."

He was deeply moved, and although he had not expected to broach the vital subject upon his mind so early as this, the opportunity which she had given him seemed too favourable to be missed.

"Gracie," he said, putting his hand on her shoulder, "you know that your happiness is everything to me— and it is for that reason . . . there is a question I must ask you . . . I hope it will not be painful for you."

"Painful?"

She smiled in surprise, and Daniel summoned all his courage.

"It is about your child, Gracie."

Without daring to lift his eyes, he felt her stiffen. After a silence, which became oppressive, she answered in a strained and altered voice: "I had hoped all that had been forgotten."

"Yes, yes," Daniel said hurriedly, fearing she would misunderstand. "No blame attaches to you. If there was a fault it was that of Henry Woodburn. But when he died, Gracie, the responsibility for that young life became yours."

She drew up and turned to face him, lips trembling. "I scarcely expected this from you, Uncle Dan. And so soon after my arrival. Don't you understand what I suffered? Father was almost out of his mind. Nisbet did not want to be burdened with a child, and I was too worn out to resist. I felt it was better for the child to be brought up on the farm near Perth where father put him, with the good country people, the Langs."

"Yes, yes, my dear," Daniel soothed her. "I know

your situation was difficult, but now you have the chance to put things right."

"It was put right at the time." She stood rigidly. "Isn't it best to leave it as it is?"

"No, no, you have a moral obligation, Gracie, and it isn't only that, it is a question of your happiness and that of your son."

"He is happy there, I know," and she added, with a touch of bitterness, "He would not remember me."

Daniel shook his head, "I tell you, your life will never be complete unless you take him back."

Again a long, heavy silence fell. She seemed to have been moved by her uncle's last words and looked at him doubtfully.

"Do you really think so, Uncle Dan?"

"I am sure of it."

"Don't you understand . . ." she stopped, blushed, and said with an effort, "I don't feel at all like that. I was forced to abandon him, to forget him. Now that part of me is dead. How could he come back . . . and love me?"

"Wouldn't he be able to love you, my dear?"

Emotion gripped the girl in spite of herself. She sighed. This suggestion, so unexpected and contrary to her plans, was very disturbing.

"We will talk about it again," she said slowly. And, resting her cheek on his shoulder, she seemed to be touched by his affection.

"You are so good to me, dearest uncle, and I am so happy to be with you again. Have I really been away for seven years? My life is beginning again. . . ."

When Daniel departed for the studio Gracie rested in her room—despite her denial the journey had fatigued her—and towards late afternoon she fell into a light sleep. But in the evening the sound of voices drew her downstairs.

Refreshed, wearing a soft gown with lace about the throat, she entered the parlour where, seated before the fireplace—now filled by a pot of spiraea—engaged in their weekly game of draughts were Daniel and Apothecary Hay.

Gracie smiled and greeted the druggist, then seated herself on the revolving piano stool, to watch the progress of the game. Somehow, from her presence, the atmosphere of the stiff Scots parlour with its formidable mahogany, its horsehair upholstery, its Highland cattle lowering from maroon walls, seemed to brighten.

For Daniel the whole room was lighter, warmer. He gazed at her from time to time with a timid happiness, not caring a whit that he was losing. And at length he said:

"Play something, Gracie."

"I'm out of practice," Gracie answered gaily in the local dialect. "Besides, Mr Hay doesn't want me to."

"I'm not minding what you do," the druggist interjected with native caution.

"Well, I will, for that," smiled Gracie. She swung round on her stool, opened the upright piano, hesitated a moment, then began to play.

It was a nice piano—a handsome wedding present to Kate from her brother Tom, which Kate, in the passion of her possessiveness, had not grudged to keep in tune. She had a special private arrangement, half-price, with the blind tuner from Shawland's in the High Street. And Gracie's touch was worthy of that instrument—Miss Gilchrist, music mistress of the Academy, had not spent her time in vain. She played one of Schubert's Impromptus. It was beautiful.

Outside the light was failing, and through the open window the mingled scent of moss roses and new-cut grass came stealing in from Daniel's garden. Gracie's figure, slender and small, had a strangely unprotected quality. Her white throat, almost luminous against her black dress, the fragility of her wrists, the very movements of her fingers had a delicate and fastidious charm.

Daniel felt his heart swell as he looked at her. Even Hay was touched as, with his long shanks outstretched and his eyes fixed sardonically upon the ceiling, he drummed the draught-board in pretended indifference.

From Schubert Gracie drifted almost idly into the traditional airs of Scotland, the native songs of her own land, until suddenly, with a glance at Daniel, she began that song he liked best of all. It was, of course, a sacred song: "*And the city hath no need of light.*"

Leaning forward, fascinated, Daniel could scarcely breathe. Gracie's voice, though small in volume, had an almost birdlike purity. It soared towards him, threading the stately melody with lovely words. It became no longer Gracie's voice but Gracie's spirit, aspiring finally towards goodness, a white soul struggling upwards through the nets of Earth. Indescribably touched, Daniel buried his face in his hands, seeing the happy vision of Gracie, reunited to her child.

The song ended, and it was as if none of them dared to move. Presently, however, the door was opened and Kate came into the room bearing a taper with which, lowering the frosted globe of the chandelier, she lit the gas. It was then that Daniel saw that Gracie's cheeks were wet with tears.

On Wednesday forenoon of the following week Daniel was in the studio, moving spryly, strapping his photographic gear in a brown canvas cover, humming cheerfully under his breath.

One of his "big days" lay ahead of him. He was going to the Academy to photograph the classes in the Elementary School, row upon row of children ranged on benches, with well-washed faces, alert and wide-eyed, in the sunny, dusty playground.

Most of Daniel's business came from this annual group work. He had most of the schools in Levenford, together with the Oddfellows, the Masons, the Bowling Club, and a score of other old-established institutions controlled by the Burgh Council.

If on a Levenford mantelpiece you saw a formidable gathering of top-hatted gentlemen and their parasol-holding ladies—say, the ceremonial opening of the new waterworks at Garshake, or the presentation of prizes at the annual Flower Show—you might be certain that in the corner of the mount would be the neat little sign: Dan'l Nimmo. Photographer. The Studio. Wellhall, Levenford.

To be sure, there was not much profit in the work,

but Daniel thoroughly enjoyed it, especially when it took him into the open air among the children. There he was in his element, happy and fussy, a regular master of ceremonies, with a stock of harmless little jokes which he was far too diffident to use upon their elders, but which unaccountably always made the children laugh. These little triumphs did much to compensate him for the exacting task of portraiture in the studio.

He was almost ready when a light tip-tapping on the glass panel of the door caused him to swing round. It was Gracie, her eyes agleam with fun, her smiling face pressed against the pane. The next instant she was in the room.

"I didn't know if I'd catch you. I hurried all the way." She breathed quickly, one hand pressed against her slender side, the other sustaining herself against his shoulder.

"Uncle Dan, I'm off for the day. Could you . . . would you cash me this small cheque?"

He gazed at her, rather taken aback, observing her "dressed-up" air, her trim costume, neat black hat and veil. Then he glanced at the cheque, which was drawn for the very modest sum of 20s.

"Where are you going?" he asked slowly.

She laughed her teasing, infectious laugh, and bent forward to sniff the rose in his button-hole. "What an inquisitive little man! And what a bonny rose! It's a nice habit you have to wear something out of your garden every day." She hesitated, then said with a rush, "Can't you guess where I'm going, Uncle Dan?"

At her tone, less than her words, Daniel's brow

cleared and his eyes kindled warmly. Six days ago he had written a long letter of explanation and inquiry to Alexander Lang at Methven Farm, near Perth. Thus far there had been no response. What was more natural than that Gracie should wish to take the trip to Perth to anticipate that reply and to see for herself how the land lay?

So, at least, Daniel construed the situation, and with ready, eager fingers he fumbled in his right-hand vest pocket. He never had any money beyond a few shillings to jingle with his keys, but from one Christmas to another, to save his face in case of necessity, he carried a single sovereign in the nickel case attached to his watch chain. Now, with a self-conscious little smile, he slipped out the gold coin and handed it over.

"Thank you, Uncle Dan," Gracie murmured. "I let myself run short of change. And I need a little for my railway fare."

Before he could reply she was out and on her way down the street, so bright and gay he had to smile in sympathy. He stood for a minute, still aglow at the thought of her present mission, then, resuming his gentle humming, bent down and began to strap up his satchel.

Down the High Street Gracie hurried, her feet light on the bone-dry pavements, until she came to the railway station. Here she bought a ticket, and, after crossing to the down line platform, entered an empty compartment in the local train for Markinch.

Presently the train clanked off, and after traversing a long tunnel drew up at Dalreoch, a poor-class outlying district of Levenford. This station, seldom used by the townspeople, now held nothing but scores of empty milk cans destined for the lochside and a solitary passenger, a man, who, hastening down the line of windows, stepped quickly into Gracie's compartment.

"Well," Gracie remarked as the train moved off again, "we managed that quite well."

David Murray gazed at her almost unwillingly, from his seat opposite, then glanced instinctively through the window as though he feared they might be observed. He was pale and restive, perhaps a little defiant. He wore a dark grey suit and a badly knotted blue tie.

So ill-tied was it that Gracie bent forward with a pretty chiding gesture and began to pat it into place. "Tch! What a careless chap he is, to be Levenford's bright young lawyer. And sulky, too. Aren't you pleased to be free of your desk for today?"

He answered perfunctorily: "Yes, yes, you know I am. But be careful, Gracie, please."

"What on earth is there to be careful about?" She sat back, mocking him gently with her eyes. "And what a frightened fellow you have turned out to be!"

He bit his moustache nervously, moodily.

"You know what people are, Gracie. Especially in Levenford. It's risky and foolish of us to take this trip."

She did not answer, but gazed distantly out of the window at the soft green landscape slowly rolling past. At length she murmured: "I love the loch so much I wanted to see it as we saw it together in the old days."

"Those days are gone, Gracie."

There was a pause. Her head remained averted, her delicate profile outlined against the window.

"Was that why you never answered the letters I wrote you from India?"

This time it was he who made no reply.

With a faint smile she turned towards him.

"And now there's Isabel, Davie. It was quite a shock when Aunt Kate told me of your engagement. Foolishly, I had always thought of you as unattached . . . and steadfast."

"Were you steadfast, Gracie?"

She did not seem to hear the question, but went on, in that same light tone.

"I remember Isabel at school. She used to wear a brown velvet dress that made her look like a prune."

"You never were very fond of the other girls, Gracie."

"No," she answered calmly. "I was more at home with the boys. Anyhow, I'm sure you'll be happy. Nisbet used to say that homely women make the best wives."

"Was that his experience?"

Her gay, infectious laugh rang out.

"That's more the David Murray I used to know."

He could not help himself, he smiled at last—his sensitive, worried smile. Somehow he had never been able to resist her. He knew it was wrong, the act of an imbecile to be here with Gracie.

When her note had come to the office suggesting this expedition he had torn it up with a frown. He had Isabel to think about, and his widowed mother, who in the most straitened circumstances had made heroic sacrifices to send him to college to take his law degree.

Besides, there was his career—he was linked now in the most favourable way with Isabel's father over the new gasworks scheme and the Burgh Causeway tenders, and a dozen other profitable ventures. He knew all this, yet here he was, taking this dangerous trip, under the very nose of a suspicious, censorious town.

But they were already at Markinch, and there was no time for further reflection. They left the train together and boarded the tiny paddle steamer that lay waiting at the pier. Almost at once the engine bell clanged, ropes were cast off, and the yellow paddles churned the green water into milky foam. Out of the little harbour they swept, then turning, throbbed steadily up the loch. It was a calm, bright day, and because it was still early in the season they had the boat almost to themselves.

When they passed the Island of Inchlade the water was so calm that the steamer's bows made no waves, but great smooth ripples which glided outward like quiet serpents. It was so still they could hear the splash of a fish a long way off, and the crisp "tchink-tchink" of a blacksmith's hammer from the village of Gielston upon the opposite shore.

Because the hills rose steeply the loch seemed deep, rich with mystery and wonder. The tiny piers at which they called were gay with budding fuschia, and the little straw-thatched whitewashed houses had the look of heavenly toys.

Leaning on the rail, Gracie laid her fingers lightly on Murray's sleeve and watched the lovely vista, like someone in a dream. Neither of them spoke, except to call attention to some aspect of the view, a patch of bracken bursting into green, a flashing waterfall among the high-up crags.

Towards noon the steamer put in at Dunbeg, its farthest port of call. Here they went ashore and walked up the single dusty street between the climbing nasturtiums on the cottage porches. The steamer would be at the pier for the next two hours, loading up with barrels of early potatoes and resting—it almost seemed—in the midday glare, waiting for the few passengers who had gone exploring in the woods.

At the end of the village, Gracie and Murray took the winding road up the hill. It was very hot, and the hum of insects filled the air. High banks of fern grew on either side, and there was a swimming, heady smell of wild thyme and sage.

They reached the summit of the hill and stood to view the loch which lay chasmed far beneath them.

"We ought to go back now. Get some lunch at the inn."

"Must we, Davie?"

"Aren't you hungry?"

She shook her head and seated herself on a patch of dry soft turf beside a clump of flowering broom.

"It's too lovely to be indoors."

After a moment's hesitation he took his place beside her. There was a silence. Then, as though meditating, she said:

"You don't know how often out there in the parched heat I thought of us, sitting here. I'm a queer creature, David. I wish I could explain . . . make you understand why things went the way they did between us. On the surface I must have seemed quite heartless . . . but underneath I cared for you a lot."

"You certainly showed it." Gazing straight ahead, he spoke from between his teeth. "You know you were in love with Woodburn."

She shook her head.

"It wasn't love, David. If anything it was pity." As he swung round abruptly and stared at her she met his eyes unflinchingly, and continued in a low and steady tone: "Henry was ill, David, far more so than anybody guessed. He'd been for months in a sanatorium without showing any improvement. One lung was riddled and the other was beginning to be affected. Oh, I admit I was carried away by his charm and his fearlessness. I had never met anyone like him before, but more than anything it was the sadness that he had so little time left that blinded me and made me want to give him something in return."

Tiny beads of sweat had broken out on Murray's brow.

"Isn't it rather late in the day for these intimate confidences?" he said in a voice that he tried to make indifferent.

"Yes, David, that's true," she answered simply, "but it is the first—and only—chance I have had."

He dared not look at her, but when he raised his eyes at last a faint smile touched her lips and her lashes fluttered. And, all caution gone, he leaned towards her with a kind of groan.

"Gracie, oh Gracie!" he whispered, losing himself in the shining of her eyes.

At five o'clock that evening, a little later than usual because of his heavy day at the Academy, Daniel returned to the studio. From a distance he saw the druggist waiting for him on the doorstep with a surprised look on his face.

"Well, it's you," said his friend. "How is Gracie?"

Daniel felt his face flush. "Gracie's very well," he replied quietly.

"No doubt, no doubt, as she was travelling today."

"And why not?" said Daniel with rising annoyance. "She had business in Perth."

The druggist shrugged. "Perth?" he said. "She was on the train to Markinch. I was on it myself."

Daniel started. He stared at Hay and slowly his heart contracted and sank within him. He could not doubt the druggist's word. Among Hay's many queer possessions he had—strange fancy in a metaphysician so desiccated—a little houseboat on Loch Lomond, a ramshackle craft anchored in Cantie Bay, about five miles above the village of Markinch.

Here, in the summer, Hay would come to spend agreeable week-ends, often taking Daniel with him for the dual purpose of argument and companionship. It was this houseboat which authenticated Hay's statement—he had told Daniel only last week that he meant to go to the loch on Wednesday "to make things ship-shape" and to leave instructions about buying in provisions.

Daniel swallowed dryly. He muttered: "Like as not Gracie changed her mind."

"To be sure," agreed Hay, cracking his bony fingers.

"Ay, ay, to be sure. No doubt that's why David Murray was with her."

"No," Daniel faltered.

The druggist answered with a pitying shrug. "I saw them take the Dunbeg boat with my own eyes."

A pang shot through Daniel. He remembered the look on Gracie's face when she came in that morning. He turned without a word, and moved slowly towards his studio. Here, as he entered the tiny lobby, he noticed a letter upon the brass salver which stood upon the hall-stand. He gazed at it dumbly.

Then, with a queer sensation of having seen it before, he picked it up. It was his own letter which he had sent to Alexander Lang at Methven Farm, near Perth. And it was marked: "*Not known. Gone away.*"

Next day the doors of the Wellhall Photographic Studio were closed. On the afternoon of that day, about four o'clock, Daniel descended from the northern express and, leaving the station with a tired, despondent air, set out towards his home.

Half-way across the common he discerned ahead of him the figure of a woman—it was his wife. From the work-bag which she carried, and the chastened angle of her head, he saw that she had been to the weekly meeting of the Church Sewing Circle. Dutifully he overtook her, and with a word of greeting they passed along the toll road together.

Daniel had been secretly to Perth to seek definite information upon the Langs, and, civilly enough, the present tenant of Methven Farm, a sturdy young countryman, had given him the facts.

Lang himself was dead these three years past; indeed, if the truth must be told, he had "drunk himself into the grave", and in the process of personal disintegration had let the farm go to rack and ruin—it had been a hard job to reclaim the wasted land. As for Mrs Lang, she was believed to have gone to the city of Winton, but no one knew for sure; she had felt her disgrace keenly and had severed all connection with her friends. There had been a child, the young farmer believed, in fact several children, for the woman had made a practice of adoption, and these, presumably, she had taken with her. But more than that he could not say.

For a moment, as he walked beside his wife, Daniel, discouraged by his fruitless expedition, had a longing to unburden himself to her. But a side glance towards her pale, resigned face deterred him. Always at the Sewing Circle was she set back upon herself, patronised by the minister's wife and the well-to-do women of the congregation, made to feel that her struggle for social recognition was futile, that all her thrift and painful endeavours, her shifts and economies, her patching and mending and polishing, were of no avail, that all, all was useless and without purpose, that she would always bear the stigma of her husband's contemptible failure, a dowdy, disappointed little woman with work-worn hands and shabby clothes, wife of a "stickit" minister.

Yet, despite her self-imposed silence, as they turned the last corner of the road an exclamation was forced from Kate's lips. Outside the front of the house stood a car, the natty little Panhard belonging to Mr Harmon, the Khedive agent.

Daniel also was visibly surprised—automobiles were rare in Levenford, and never before had one stood at his gate. They both hastened their steps towards the house.

As they entered the hall there came from the parlour a deep masculine voice followed by Gracie's laugh, that individual, provoking, fascinating laugh. With her mittened hand Kate pushed open the door. Frank Harmon, very smart in a short covert coat and check waistcoat, his yellow dogskin driving gloves resting on his well-creased knees, was reclining in the best armchair, smooth, smiling and expansive, with a glass of sherry in his strong fingers and a plate of biscuits at his elbow. On a low stool, not far from the chair, wearing one of her nicest muslin afternoon gowns, sat Gracie. Her own glass of sherry stood on a little table beside her.

The situation was so unexpected, so intimate and complete, Kate scarcely knew how to meet it. On the one hand it outraged her to find Gracie playing hostess in her sacred parlour, carelessly dispensing sherry —which was never used except on the most ceremonious occasions—and actually drinking the wine herself. Yet upon the other it gratified her pride to be visited by a person of Harmon's standing. Not only was the agent a man of means—it was said he had extensive holdings in the Khedive Company—but he went about largely in Levenford society, dined at Sir John Ralston's, for instance, and was generally much sought after. A faint spot of colour had risen from Kate's earthy cheeks. In her embarrassment she cleared her throat.

The sound caused Gracie to turn her head and immediately she was on her feet, her expression gay and smiling, in no way discomposed.

"Aunt Kate . . . Uncle Dan . . . you know Mr Harmon. He called on me this afternoon, and as he doesn't drink tea I offered him this little refreshment. May I pour you a glass?"

"No, thank you," Kate could not forbear an acid compression of her lips. "I would not dream of partaking in the afternoon."

"Sherry is surely a mild tipple, m'm," Harmon protested heartily. "Why, out East . . ." Here it seemed as though a warning glance from Gracie restrained him. He broke off, took up a biscuit, and crunched it amicably between his strong white teeth.

"I understand you knew our niece in India," Kate remarked more pleasantly

"Yes, indeed, m'm," Harmon agreed courteously, "though less well than I would have wished. My visits to Calcutta were never prolonged. But your niece's bungalow was always an oasis for the traveller on such occasions."

"Oh, Frank," cried Gracie with laughing eyes, "you are a wicked flatterer. But I forgive you because you are such a dear, kind friend."

Her tone, excited and a little unrestrained, caused Kate and Daniel to gaze at her more attentively. Daniel in particular was perplexed and somewhat troubled to find Gracie suddenly upon such terms of "first name" intimacy with the Khedive agent. Harmon had the reputation of a gay bachelor, a ladies' man, and there were one or two queer stories concerning him—perhaps merely the sort of small town gossip likely to be connected with a man not native to the district, who travelled a great deal, coming and going without warning, and whose local establishment consisted of a suite of rooms at the Castle Hotel. Beyond the fact that he had once found him savagely beating a springer dog for some misdemeanour, Daniel knew nothing wrong of the man, yet he shrank from him, as from something evil.

"Frank has offered me a job in the Khedive office." Gracie made the announcement with a more than usual display of feeling. "Good hours and generous pay. Isn't that sweet of him?"

"Indeed it is," said Kate with a quick breath of satisfaction.

"Not at all," Harmon protested easily. "Only too happy to be of service." He glanced at his watch, a fine gold hunter, and stood up. "Now, if you'll excuse me, I have an appointment at the shipyard. When the warm days come, Mrs Nimmo, you must let me drive you to the loch. My little runabout goes very well . . . I'll guarantee we don't break down."

He shook hands all round, very massive and agreeable, then pulled on his gloves. Daniel showed him to the door and, when the chugging of the machine had died away, stood a moment to readjust his thoughts.

It was good, yes, splendid that Gracie should have settled work. He must not let his dislike of Harmon colour his judgement. This was the first essential step towards the reorganisation of Gracie's life. As to the next, he, Daniel, must ensure its achievement. After all, some initial difficulty was only to be expected, and the setback which he had experienced in Perth was anything but final. There were other avenues of approach open to him—he would advertise in the Winton newspapers, offer a reward, even write to the chief constable of the county.

At these reflections he felt more confident, pervaded by a slow resurgence of optimism and resource. At all costs he would find Gracie's child, the one instrument which would stabilise his wayward, his beloved niece. Turning, he went back briskly to the parlour.

Here Kate had already removed evidence of the unprecedented repast. Only the decanter remained, having been returned, reproachfully it seemed, to its place of state upon the chiffonier.

It was, in fact, more than half-empty and as he studied, absently, its seriously depleted state, the suspicion suddenly crossed Daniel's mind that Gracie must surely have taken more than the single glass which courtesy required of her. He glanced towards her quickly. With flushed cheeks and bright eyes she had gone to the piano and was playing a lively waltz.

Chapter III

THE WEATHER CONTINUED fine for several weeks and July came in with a blaze of solar heat. Awnings appeared over the windows of the town and the watering cart went round the cobbled streets.

One Friday night towards the middle of the month David Murray was working late in his office in Church Street. It was not a large office, but it had a certain solid and well-established air. The high desk was of fine mahogany, bound by a heavy brass rail, and the old-fashioned safe set deep into the wall seemed strong enough to stand a siege. Two windows, opening into Church Wynd, were masked by a dark gauze screen on which was painted, in faded gilt, Waldie and Waldie, Solicitors. The same name, almost polished out, was upon the brass doorplate.

The firm had been founded by Archibald Waldie more than 50 years before, then carried on for some time by Alexander, his son. Alex, however, had shown a strong inclination towards commerce, had taken up contracting in lieu of law practice, and succeeded beyond all expectations. This, in the first instance, had given Murray an opportunity.

David's career as a law student had been brilliant. He had neither money nor standing—his father, who died when he was young, had been merely the janitor of the Burgh Hall—but Davie had that inestimable quality of the Scots youth, not merely brains, but also application. He won every scholarship open to him and took his degree with first-class honours. And then, from being merely "articled", came his chance, without payment of a premium, with Waldie and Waldie.

For three years now Davie Murray had managed the law business, and with his engagement to Waldie's daughter, Isabel, recently announced, it was common knowledge that he would succeed to it, and to other things as well.

Davie, with his quick, dark, open face, his eagerness to please, his endless diligence, was liked by everyone. "Yes," Alex Waldie would frequently remark, with a mixture of complacency and patronage, "our Davie's a glutton for work."

At present, however, Murray seemed to find concentration difficult. He had a task to do, the desk was littered with the monthly returns of the County Water Board, yet his thoughts were far away from figures.

With a nervous frown he sat tangling his black hair with his fingers—a habit of his student years—and thinking, yes, thinking of Gracie. Why, oh why, had he let himself get mixed up with her again? It really was not wise, in fact, it was devilish stupid. And yet, she was so sweet, so bonnie, she lifted a man's heart right out of his body, she was really the only woman he had ever loved.

At their secret stolen meetings it was like living in another world where money, position, prospects, where, indeed, his whole career, did not matter a brass farthing beside the tender shining of her eyes.

Murray groaned, and his gaze strayed to the cabinet photograph of Isabel Waldie in its new silver frame, planted on the desk directly before him. He bit his pen with a deepening frown. Yet David was not really looking at the photograph. He was looking at himself, and the image that he saw was hardly the popular picture he habitually presented to the town.

In Murray there were two personalities, and they lived in ever-growing conflict—the one sensitive, intense, utopian, the other a shrewd and calculating character determined to succeed at any cost. At the university Murray had read the verse of Robert Tannahill and led the Fabian Society debates. Now, though he still sported his old Fabian tie occasionally, he had others of more sedate hue which he wore when meeting the bailies at the local burgh council or when sitting in conference with Alex Waldie over plans for the new Knoxhill Gas Company.

Bitterly, and often with the self-analysis that troubles such a man, Murray told himself that he had the soul of a poet and the heart of an adventurer. He lacked the qualities of a businessman, the application which would gain him the praise of Waldie and his friends. He hated the smiling deference and the favours that were reserved for the nabobs of the little town, and despised their petty intrigues. But how could he resist taking his share of the good things that were offered? Calculating and shrewd, he knew how to work to his own advantage. But as soon as he could afford it, he would return to the delights of poetry.

With a cry of disgust, Murray threw down his pen—he could not do any more work tonight. At that moment he heard a step and Alex Waldie came in briskly.

"I thought I would find you working," he said. "It is time to shut up shop."

Murray lowered his eyes for fear of giving himself away.

"I was just stopping."

"That's good. Too much work is bad for the spirits. Come on, then. My car is outside and they are waiting for us at home."

Murray, his face expressionless, began to arrange his papers while Waldie walked up and down. He was a square, heavy man with a pock-marked face and sly little eyes. He found it impossible to keep still.

Davie was ready at last and the two men left the office. Outside, the heat of the day had given place to a pleasant cool. Waldie tucked the rug with ostentatious friendliness round Murray's knees and they drove off in his gig towards Knoxhill.

Once or twice it seemed as if, beneath his joviality, he flashed an acute and surreptitious glance at his silent companion. But outwardly he was more cordial than ever. And presently he remarked in an intimate tone:

"Our 'pauchie' with Langloan is going through all right."

A shadow of distaste passed over Murray's face, but he nodded his head in agreement.

"The deeds will be up for signature tomorrow."

"Good work, Davie!" complimented Waldie.

David said nothing.

The "pauchie"—a Scottish euphemism for a twisty stroke of business—referred to the purchase of 70 acres of land which would, in the Lord's good time, become the site of the new gas works. Langloan, the hard-working market gardener to whom the land belonged, was selling it for an old song. Murray, as Waldie's agent, was the purchaser.

Soon the land would multiply in value by twenty times at least, and Murray would profit handsomely in the subsequent disbursement. Waldie, as sponsor of the coming scheme, would see to that. Here was the advantage, Murray thought with sudden bitterness, of the patronage of his prospective father-in-law.

Alexander Waldie was, without doubt, a good man to stand in with; he had his thumb upon most of the affairs of Levenford, and, overflowing the royal burgh, his interests extended to several terraces of houses in Dalreoch. He had also a couple of tramp steamers coasting down to Campbeltown, a controlling share in the Leven tannery, in the dye works in Darroch and the saw-mill at Garshake.

As distinguished from the goods in which he dealt, which were often of the worst, Waldie had a motto for his own possessions, "Nothing but the best". And his house—a grey sandstone affair in the Scots baronial style, surrounded by a gravelled terrace and circular beds of red geraniums—expressed this opulent philosophy to the full.

Within, the furniture was massive. The dining-room especially, into which Waldie led Murray immediately on their arrival, was distinguished by a ponderous sideboard reaching almost to the ceiling, two huge stags' heads—not shot by Waldie—upon the wall, a set of chairs specially carved in black walnut, and a heavy table of the same wood, already set for supper.

Despite this formidable magnificence Waldie, like many another self-made man, made a virtue of his plainness. "Take us as you find us" was his favourite phrase, and tonight, in his usual blunt fashion, he did not stand on ceremony.

"Are you ready for us, woman?" he called out to his wife, then explained to David, with a smile, "They'll be upstairs at their titivating."

Almost immediately, however, Isabel and her mother came down. And when the usual greetings had passed Waldie rubbed his hands and chuckled.

"Come away now, Davie! We'll sit in and have a bite!"

The "bite" was less supper than a late high tea—the main dish was a fine cut of salmon, flanked by a saddle of lamb and a cold boiled ham. In addition, there were ample supplies of bread, toast and scones, a plateful of oatcakes, another of pastries and yet another of shortbread, a large wedge of cheese, a barrel of biscuits, and, finally, a shuddering pink blancmange. Enough food lay upon the table—and Waldie often remarked the fact—to feed an ordinary family for a week. And now, as he set about it, he kept genially exhorting Murray to do the same.

Despite his abstraction, David was not unaware that the contractor was more expansive than usual in his manner, and his wife considerably less so. There was a watchful, a "put-out" look on Mrs Waldie's homely face, and she sat very upright in her chair with an air rather different from her ordinary fond indulgence. She answered his remarks without enthusiasm and seemed alert for even his slightest lapse.

"Pass the vinegar to Mr Waldie, David!" Her voice held an unaccustomed inflection of reproach.

Isabel, on the other hand, was more openly affectionate than ever. She wore a new blue dress, cut low at the neck, with an edging of fichu upon the short sleeves. It was clear she had taken a great deal of trouble with her appearance and had liberally besprinkled herself with the new perfume, Jockey Club. In her manner there was all the coyness of an affianced young woman, and her doll-like blue eyes languished possessively upon David whenever he glanced across at her. He had a suspicion that her hand, lingering beneath the table, was ready to link with his.

"You haven't tried the shortbread," she pouted. "I made it specially for you."

He took a piece, and a flush of gratification flooded her face. Murray, in spite of himself, was touched. He had no conceit. He felt suddenly that her fondness for him was something which he should prize. Although not endowed with grace or wit, she was a sensible girl of a safe, conventional pattern, not unattractive, really, with her high colour and plump figure. Tonight, because of the way she had done her hair, her features lost their heaviness and her mouth its petulant droop.

"Isabel's a rare hand at the shortbread." The contractor gave an approving nod as he helped himself.

"Yes," Mrs Waldie agreed. "*Her* baking never gives me the wind!"

Isabel's expression changed and, conscious of the vulgarity, she glanced at her mother with annoyance. That worthy woman was always offending her daughter's sense of refinement.

This refinement of Isabel's was peculiar, a queer physical reaction which affected her when she was confronted even by the minor indelicacies of life, by the use of words like sweat and saliva, even in their proper context, by the hair on the back of her father's hands as he reached out to pat her, by anything even remotely gross.

For a long time she had yearned to be in love and had tried to care for various young men of Levenford, who, because of her father's position, readily paid court to her. But in each case the physical reaction intervened. Young Edward Mowat, the minister's son, deemed an admirable match, had displeased her because he always had a frost of dandruff on his coat collar. Mungo Crawford, student of medicine and successor to his father's practice, had been banished because once when he kissed her he placed his tongue against her lips. As to young Dickie, Isabel, alone in the sanctuary of her bedroom, had rocked herself to and fro in cosmic anguish: "Oh dear, oh dear! The very *odour* of him sickens me!"

And then came Davie Murray, pleasant, handsome, and "nice". Here, however carefully she might seek—

ah, here was nothing to revolt her. And so, free of her obsession, Isabel made of Davie the paragon. The true Sir Launcelot. She pined in his absence, hung upon his words, basked in the sunshine of his smile.

Tonight, however, Davie had few smiles for her. The suspicion was growing upon him that something hidden and impending hung above the groaning board. Indeed, when they had finished, an imperceptible interchange of glances took place between Waldie and his wife. Mrs Waldie rose:

"Come, Isabel! We'll let your father and David have their smoke. They'll join us in the parlour later."

"But, mother," Isabel protested with a drooping lip, "I'd rather stop with David."

"Tut, tut," Waldie intervened, eyeing his daughter with affectionate remonstrance. "You can spare him for a minute, surely."

"Then let me light his cigar," Isabel pouted. She fetched over the big silver box and made quite a ceremony of it, forgetting that Waldie also wished to smoke, until her mother's reproving voice rang out from the door. "Your father, Isabel, *if you please*."

When the two men were alone, Waldie, his cigar between his moist lips, winked at David, very jovial and masculine, and produced the whisky from the sideboard. He poured a stiff tot for each of them, then lay back with a sigh, surrounded by the remnants of the feast, a well-fed citizen, his fingers twiddling the gold chain on his projecting paunch, his foot swinging rhythmically beneath the table.

"Well, here's to us." He brought out his usual toast, adding before he drank, "Who's like us!"

There was a pause while Waldie drew his breath in over the spirits, audibly, reflectively.

"You know, Davie," he exclaimed suddenly, "I'm very fond of Isabel. She's a nice lass!"

Murray received his glass awkwardly.

"Come to that," Waldie went on, "I'm fond of you yourself, lad. Now, now, don't interrupt me. I mean what I say. And I'm glad to see you getting on. Mind you, though maybe I shouldn't mention the fact, it was I who gave you your start. And if you handle yourself properly, with me behind you, there's no knowing to what heights you may go." He lowered his voice seductively. "After all, this law business is only a means to an end. You and I could be partners, Davie, in time, if we matched our steps up the hill together!"

Murray, eyes still fixed on the tablecloth, made an indistinct murmur of gratitude, and his heart beat a trifle faster at the thought.

"You see," Waldie continued in a guileless voice, "my lass is in love with you, Davie. She wants you. And she's our ewe lamb you understand, I wouldn't have her disappointed for all the gold in China. That's why"—Waldie smiled and poured more whisky for each of them—"that's why I was upset by a piece of information that came my way today."

Murray felt his pulse miss a beat.

"What information?"

"I may as well be candid with you, Davie. I heard that you're carrying on with that Lindsay woman."

Murray, though scarcely taken by surprise, reddened to the roots of his hair. He answered hurriedly, defensively:

"You know what a place Levenford is for gossip."

"Ay, ay, I know," Waldie answered with a sympathetic laugh which caused Murray's flush to deepen. His lips twitched back in a nervous grimace.

"It's a complete exaggeration. I've only seen her once or twice."

Waldie laughed again.

"Of course. There's not a grain of truth in it. The idea! But mind you, it wasn't exactly pleasant hearing for me. And of course I had to mention it to the wife. Needless to say, Isabel doesn't know a word of it."

"I'm glad of that." Davie kept his eyes averted and something made him add: "Although it's so damned absurd."

"Ay, ay, damned absurd," agreed Waldie smoothly. "But still I had to speak to you about it. You see, the remedy's so simple."

There was a pause, then Murray lifted his head, meeting the contractor's gaze with a struggle, a great effort. Behind the unctuous merriment, the jovial good fellowship in those deep-set eyes, he sensed a sudden challenge, a menace it was impossible to ignore.

"What remedy?" he muttered.

"Just this, Davie man," said Waldie slowly. "That we fix the day of the wedding." His teeth were together firmly, but his voice, dropping out the words, was smooth as oil. "When will we put up the banns?"

Murray's fingers stiffened round his glass. He saw it

all—how Waldie had led him on under the bland pretence of belief in his denials. Damnation! He was no simpleton, the bold contractor, he knew, and no mistake! And now the threat behind his pleasantry was unmistakable. He loved his Isabel. Heaven help the man who failed her.

For a moment David sat in sullen silence, then, all at once, his mood turned upside down and he had an hysterical impulse to laugh. It was all so idiotic. Did Waldie think he would run away? Didn't he realise that their interests were bound together inseparably?

Yes, yes, his whole future lay with Waldie, the road to power and fortune. He couldn't give it up. There was no reason for him to hesitate. Why should he concern himself with Gracie Lindsay? She had betrayed him with Woodburn, had married Nisbet Vallance, she could be nothing to him now: she was less than nothing, a slightly damaged character for all her charm and beauty, a woman upon whom the eyes of the world would always rest with misgiving and distrust.

In a flash his mind was made up. He lifted his glass and drained it. Without flinching he met Waldie's eye. "The sooner you put up the banns the better it suits me."

There was a brief silence while Waldie's eyes searched Murray's face. Then slowly the contractor's smile broadened. Gently he patted Murray on the back.

"I knew you were a good lad, Davie. We'll have the wedding come September." Rising, he linked his arm with David's. "Come away now, and we'll tell the ladies."

It was the following evening, and Gracie had finished her day's work at the Khedive Line offices. Preparatory to her departure she stood before the small mirror above her desk adjusting her hat with the coquettish gestures of a pretty woman.

The office boy and the senior clerk had already gone, but Gracie, with an hour to spare before six o'clock, had no need of haste. In leisurely fashion she picked up her gloves and was moving towards the door when the bell rang from Mr Harmon's room. She paused, turned and went in.

Harmon was in his swing chair, with his feet up and a newly-lighted cigar between his full lips. He smiled at her in a friendly manner, and moved his bulky frame from its position of ease.

"Oh, Gracie," he exclaimed, "I wondered if they'd telephoned me from the shipyard this afternoon?"

"No, indeed. If they had I should certainly have let you know."

"Good. You're picking up the job very quickly. You don't find it too difficult?"

"Not a bit. I used to type out reports for Nisbet."

Harmon smiled indulgently. He gazed at her, secretly gloating over the lines of her graceful body. She had never been more beautiful, and there was a brightness in her eyes that he had never seen before.

"Were you happy with him?" he asked softly.

She hesitated for a moment. "Fairly happy."

"Fairly happy!" his smile deepened. "Marriage is a lottery, my dear."

Then, as she did not answer:

"In any case, I hope you are happy here . . . do you understand me?"

"Yes, Frank. You are very kind."

"Not at all. In one way, our situations are similar. We have both travelled the world and now we have to live in this grubby little town."

"Oh, no!" she protested. "It isn't like that."

He laughed.

"Wait and you'll see. I could not stay here myself unless I was able to escape from time to time. You know I travel a lot, combining business with pleasure. This autumn I am going to Spain. It is a charming country. I recommend it for the time when you are bored with life here."

He stopped suddenly, as if struck by a happy thought, and glanced at the clock.

"Time is getting on. Why don't we have a drive? One can't breathe here. And we could have dinner at the Markinch Arms."

Masculine attentions always pleased her, and she had waited for this invitation for several days. However, she shook her head and smiled.

"I am sorry, Frank, but I am already engaged this evening."

Except that his heavy brows contracted slightly, his expression did not change. He examined his finger-nails, which were closely and carefully trimmed.

"A man?"

She countered gaily. "Am I one to go out with women?"

"Who is he, then? A handsome stranger?"

"In this wretched little town?" She parodied his words. "Don't be absurd, Frank."

He drew on his cigar, placated.

"Well, in that case I shan't insist. But don't forget, as a friend I have a very definite interest in you. I shall count on you for another evening."

She made a playful gesture of reproof, her smile still brightly noncommittal. She was not unaware of the sensual gleam in his apparently benignant eye, yet she felt that she could always handle men of Frank Harmon's type. Or any man, for that matter. She had had so many of them at her feet.

A few minutes later, walking along the High Street, she decided she would not go home to tea. In a resigned fashion Kate had been difficult lately, for what reason Gracie could not guess; and Daniel, still bent upon his search, was absent, somewhat distant in his manner. Gracie did not wish to dampen that sense of freedom and expectation which now swelled within her breast.

Indeed, ever since Daniel had raised the matter, Gracie had refused, subconsciously yet stubbornly, to lend herself to his intention. The episode with Woodburn was an act of folly which she had buried in the past and now had no desire to resurrect.

The child, removed by her father before she had even seen it, meant nothing to her; and she, of course, could mean nothing to the child, for whom other ties and loyalties had now been forged. Why should she disturb a situation well settled and adjusted, break up the healing tissues which time had slowly formed around this wound?

No, she would not, now especially, when she had won back Murray's love and so could build her future on a happy marriage. Nothing must interfere with that.

Daniel, she was confident, would soon tire of his wild-goose chase and be content to leave things as they were . . . or rather, as she felt they would be, when her hopes materialised and the true flowering of her individuality had come to pass.

The town was quite deserted: it was that zero hour when the Yard "was out" and the children at their lessons, when most housewives were "busy with the dishes", when nobody—beyond a few old men and a stray dog at the Cross—was in the streets. Gracie did not mind. She took her ease by idling before the shops.

At Paton's, the bookseller's a few doors down, she went in and bought a newspaper, the *Levenford Advertiser*. She might have stopped a moment to pass the time of day with Eliza Paton, still the same Miss Paton, with her high sateen blouse and net fringe, who in the old days had been reputed a great "reader" and a noted "recommender" of a novel from her small but select circulating library. Yet Miss Paton, for some reason, was in no mood to talk with Gracie. She answered with civility, but was gone quickly from her counter.

Why did she look at me like that? thought Gracie, puzzled, as she left the shop. Oh well, never mind! She dismissed it with a smile. Perhaps Eliza was in the middle of the latest thriller, and anxious to know if the man with the moustache was really a count.

Still with that same tenderness touching the corners of her mouth, Gracie turned down Clydeview Road, and, passing through the eastern outskirts of Levenford, she came at length to the foot of Dumbreck Hill.

Here, with the wide estuary of the river in front and the park-like land of Dumbreck estate behind her, she might have been miles from any sign of the town, and with a sigh of contentment she sat down on the low stone wall which bordered the roadway. This was their usual meeting-place, and David would be here at any minute now. She looked at her watch. Perhaps she was a little early. Yet she did not mind the wait.

Absently, she was conscious of her mood as being particularly and exquisitely happy, like a physical delight within the centre of her being. Things were going right for her at last.

Dreamily she planned ahead, thinking of the home which she would make, of how she would help David to a better career than ever he could have with Isabel Waldie. She would cultivate people for his sake, steer him into a Crown appointment, a judgeship, and finally to Parliament.

She took off her hat and let the sun beat upon her bare head. Even in that light her skin was so fine that the brightness of the evening enhanced its beauty. Her colouring, already warm, was illuminated by the setting sun, and she had an air, a quality of style, which was individual, her own. A little brown scarf, for instance, which she had wound round her throat, gave to her a piquancy, a queer fastidious charm far beyond the value of the simple stuff.

And she had, above everything, such freshness. Gazing at her, perched upon that old wall, one felt that she might walk for 20 miles along these dusty roads in this summer heat and never lose a whit of her cool spruceness, but would still be neat and smiling, full of that secret and inexhaustible vitality at the end of it.

But meanwhile, David was late, he must have had difficulty in getting away, and in idle fashion she began to glance through her paper, which, indeed, she had bought with some such idea of passing the time. Like Miss Paton, it had changed little—the same advertisements and announcements, the same sonorous and stately promulgations: "Interest in the burgh is again being aroused by the forthcoming Flower Show . . ."

Gracie looked at her watch again. Goodness! David *was* late—half-an-hour now! And there was still no sight of his dark, hastening figure on the long white stretch of road. A tiny cloud of perplexity gathered behind Gracie's eyes.

She turned over the paper, trying to find some item of news to interest her. Then, all at once, she saw the paragraph. It was not a large paragraph—though it took due precedence at the head of a column of local gossip which had existed from time immemorial under the heading "Jottings by the Way"—yet it seemed to leap from the printed page, to strike at her with malicious, frightful violence. It was the intimation that David and Isabel Waldie would be married at the parish church on the first day of September.

Gracie stared at the paragraph, her whole body suddenly motionless, as though she had forgotten how to breathe. Her gaze travelled swiftly up the deserted road, then swiftly fell.

She began, without knowing it, to fold the paper into a small, tight square. When it would fold no further she pressed it stupidly between her hands. A moment passed and then a thought struck her. She rose hurriedly, as if ashamed that someone might find her waiting there, waiting patiently for a man who would never arrive. She set off, her head lowered, back the way that she had come.

As she entered the town and gradually approached the Cross there were more people in the streets, and of those quite a few turned to look after her. But Gracie was unconscious of their stares. Her mind was whirling, whirling in a giddy haze of doubt and pain. Yes, yes, a mistake. Some stupid rumour had been printed, that was all. It wasn't true. Davie simply could not do a thing like this: he was hers, he always had been hers. She lifted her head, her breathing coming faster. Instinctively she hastened her pace. Four minutes later she crossed Church Wynd and ran direct, through the side door, into Murray's office.

"Davie," she cried, "I had to come and find you."

He started at the sight of her. Seated there with his elbows on his desk and the fine silver photograph in front of him, he changed colour and his eyes dropped to the paper which she still held clenched in her right hand. For a minute neither of them spoke, then Murray, angered at his own weakness, made an effort to collect himself.

"You shouldn't have come here, Gracie. I'm busy."

Under the soft muslin of her blouse her breast gave

a small, convulsive movement like a bird struggling to be free.

"I waited and waited for you at Dumbreck."

"Well!" His eyes evaded hers. There was a pause. "You know how it is. There's no need to make a fuss."

"Davie!" She reached out her hand to him as if to capture something he had withdrawn. "Why do you talk to me that way? And why didn't you tell me . . . properly?"

"You knew everything there was to tell." He spoke stiffly, sullenly, his gaze still fixed upon the floor. "Long before you came back I was engaged to Isabel Waldie. And now I'm going to marry her."

"But what about you and me, Davie? We've always belonged to each other, really and truly, since the very beginning, in spite of all the wrong and stupid things that happened. Isabel isn't the wife for you. Don't you remember what you said at Dunbeg?"

"That was midsummer madness," he went on, defending himself. "Besides, you know how I was placed. It was asking for trouble."

"Then you don't care for me, Davie?" she asked, her voice low. "You know I'm fond of you."

He raised his head at last and looked at her. She was so pretty, in his dull, old office, yes, even prettier in her distress, that his anger and compunction deepened. He hated and despised himself. And because of that he wished to hurt her more. He said:

"That's just it, Gracie. You get fond of men too easily."

She drew back as if he had struck her in the face.

Her eyes, fixed upon him, showed the hurt his words gave her. Her face darkened, and despite herself, her voice rose.

"I see what you mean. A very pretty, gentlemanly, remark. And after I'd given my word I loved you."

"I don't believe you," he answered doggedly. "Nor would anybody else in Levenford. No, no! Your reputation's not exactly healthy here. Oh, damn it all! Why do I have to argue with you? I've got my own position to look to. I can't afford to get mixed up with anything not above board. We must never see each other again. It's all over and finished between us."

"I see . . . you're a public figure now, Davie. Likely you'll be Provost one day. You couldn't be mixed up with the likes of me." Her voice, quivering with passionate scorn, echoed through the office.

"For God's sake, don't speak so loud." Nervously he glanced towards the inner door. "I've people waiting . . . Mrs Stott and the minister's wife."

"What do I care? Let them all hear what a miserable, cheap, petty coward you are. If I made a mistake, at least it was a generous one. I didn't sell myself for a partnership in a law office."

"Gracie . . . the whole street'll hear you."

"How much did you get with her, Davie? Be sure you take it in gilt-edged bonds. . . ."

Scalding, bitter tears broke from her eyes, she sobbed convulsively, and thinking only of escape went wildly through the front waiting-room, unconscious of the women who sat there.

When she had gone Murray remained stiff and pale,

staring at the empty space before him. Suddenly, with a violent gesture, he took up the paper-weight on his desk as though to hurl it against the wall. But he checked himself. Composing his features, he rose to admit the two clients who were waiting for him.

About a week later, towards four o'clock on a grey Saturday afternoon, Kate Nimmo sat at home alone—Gracie was out and Daniel had again departed upon one of these trips which were proving an increasing source of disappointment to him and of irritation to herself.

There was, indeed, upon Kate's face a faint unconscious frown, and it deepened at her thoughts. She was not satisfied with the way things were going in her hitherto well-regulated household. Still less was she pleased with the rumours which reached her from the town.

At that moment the front doorbell rang. In some surprise, for she was little used to visitors, Kate rose to answer it. And there, upon her doorstep, stood the tall angular figure of Mrs Mowat, the minister's wife.

"I happened to be this way," Susan Mowat remarked, "I thought I might call."

"How kind of you," Kate replied. "Won't you come in?"

Although her tone was polite, Kate's nerves had drawn together tensely, and as she led the way into the parlour she felt a warm patch of colour mounting on her cheek. The minister's wife was everything that she, Kate Nimmo, might have been—mistress of the manse, arbiter of the destinies of the Sewing Circle and the monthly Table Teas, a personage of high social consequence in the town. Kate's unobtrusive bosom had no great capacity for envy. But the other woman, with her sharp tongue and patronising ways, had often wounded Kate, and so aroused in her a deep antipathy.

"I trust you are well," said Kate with false brightness when Susan was seated. "And your husband."

"The minister," said Mrs Mowat, gravely repudiating familiarity, "is well."

Silence. By all the rules of Levenford etiquette the visitor should now have made inquiry for the husband of her hostess, but Susan Mowat did not do so, and the omission cut Kate to the quick. Hiding her vexation under a pretence of sprightliness she declared:

"Isn't the weather glorious for the time of year? Daniel was remarking yesterday it's the finest July he can remember. I must say his sweet peas are looking wonderful."

"Hmm!" said Susan Mowat briefly. She placed her gold-rimmed pince-nez on her long, bony nose and glanced round the room as though seeking signs of deficiency or neglect.

"Is he still holding these open-air prayer meetings at Dalreoch?"

The spot of red burned deeper into the earthy colour of Kate's cheek. With a great effort she managed to answer reasonably.

"Yes, he still goes there. It's his way of labouring in the vineyard. Humble work, maybe! But it's the Lord's work none the less."

Another silence. Kate struggled with her temper, reminding herself how fatal it would be to lose it. No, no, she must not let herself get touchy. Perhaps she was exaggerating. Or even imagining things. And, after all, surely the social importance of Susan Mowat's call was sufficiently gratifying to enable her to withstand any little slights or snubs. She forced a hospitable smile.

"You'll drink a dish of tea with me?"

"I'm obliged to you," Mrs Mowat shook her head. "But I am here for another reason. Is your niece at home?"

"No, she's out."

"Hmm!" Again that same portentous sound escaped Susan Mowat's lips. "She's out a good deal, I should fancy."

"Gracie likes getting about," explained Kate.

"Indeed." A cold smile twisted Susan Mowat's lips. "Provided she has somebody to get about with."

Kate felt herself losing her presence of mind. Her heart, which often bothered her, and which in fact she knew to be weak, began to thump heavily in her side. She wished, all at once, that she were upstairs quietly lying down, that she had pretended to be out, that she had not let Susan Mowat into the house at all. She said, weakly:

"That's just the old story they hold against Gracie."

"The old story!" exclaimed Susan Mowat disdainfully. She drew herself accusingly erect. "Kate Nimmo, unpleasant though it may be, I have something I find it my duty to tell you. It's a matter of common knowledge all over the town that your niece Gracie has been misconducting herself with David Murray, trying to break up his engagement with Isabel Waldie."

Kate's labouring heart gave an extra jump. "I can't believe it," she protested.

"Indeed!" The minister's wife answered with the utmost scorn. "But the whole town believes it. They were seen at Markinch, and several times at Dumbreck. And I myself heard Davie, poor lad, showing her the door."

She paused triumphantly, head thrown back, elbows squared. "You surely know that Gracie Lindsay always was a bold brazen hussy, from her earliest days at the Academy. And now she's come back she's worse by far. I could tell you a thing or two if I chose to open my mouth, what she's up to now, for instance, but I'll never have it said of me that I spread scandal, no, no, but only that I stopped it, and that's why I'm here today, Kate Nimmo."

All out of breath she made another pause, for one shuddering inspiration, before rushing on.

"You know yourself that your husband has always doted on Gracie Lindsay, mooning over her at the Bible Class when her skirts were hardly below her knees. Baillie Waldie was recalling it to the minister only yesterday. It's all very well to say she was a schoolgirl then. She's not a schoolgirl now. Ever since she's been back he's been moonstruck, letting her run in and out of his studio at all hours, taking her arm as they come across the common."

The last insinuation was, Kate knew, completely false. And yet it crushed her. Daniel was such a fool anyone might draw damaging conclusions from his actions. Kate could not think coherently, and for the moment, at least, the fight had gone out of her. All the colour had vanished from her face, leaving it quite grey. She sat helplessly while the minister's wife rose and, pulling on her gloves with sharp forceful tugs, delivered herself of her final words.

"I'm sorry I've had to speak my mind this way, Kate Nimmo, but my duty was clear to me. Maybe you can still do something about it. That remains to be seen. But I'll tell you one thing plain. We have young people to think of and protect, decent God-fearing young men like my son and his companions. So if you don't take steps to stop this open scandal in the town, then believe me, others will!"

Kate made no reply. Still in a kind of daze she saw Susan Mowat throw her a last pitying look, then turn and sweep majestically from the room. Not, to save her life, could Kate have moved. Only when the front door slammed did she comprehend fully that her visitor had gone.

That sound brought her out of her stupefaction. She shivered as though an icy shower had struck her, and a slow wave of indescribable emotion passed over her. For perhaps the first time she realised exactly what had been said.

That she should be so spoken to in her own house, and by Susan Mowat of all people! Wave after wave swept upon her—pain, bitterness and humiliation—oh, humiliation most of all!

It was not that she believed the accusation levelled

against Daniel. She knew him too well—indeed, she loved him too well—to believe him capable of that! But it was enough that in his fondness he had given occasion for the clacking of slanderous tongues. And was it merely fondness? He had "doted" on Gracie all her life, the minister's wife had said. A pang of jealousy tore at Kate's breast.

As for Gracie—coming here uninvited with her pretty, wheedling ways and her smooth, smiling face—she was the root and branch of all the trouble. Dark anger rose up in Kate's heart, forcing glittering tears into her eyes. She rose and went into the kitchen. She would show Gracie, yes, and Daniel too. She was not a woman to be used in such a fashion.

"Gracie!" she called out suddenly in an unnatural voice.

There was no answer. Gracie was not back yet.

Going to the window, Kate seated herself there, her bosom rising and falling. Her hands clenched nervously as she waited.

The twilight was falling when Gracie returned. She came through the gate. The front door opened with scarcely a sound and she stood in the lobby, her expression pensive, her figure relaxed, as though she were fatigued.

She remained an instant there, then removed her light coat and silently advanced along the passage with the intention, it seemed, of reaching her own room unobserved. But she had taken only a few paces before she drew up, aware that Kate stood at the foot of the staircase blocking her way.

"It's you, Aunt Kate. You quite startled me."

Kate did not answer. She stood there, one hand gripping the stair banister, the other pressed hard against her side. Her face was indistinct, yet it looked stony amongst the shadows of the lobby, and her body was oddly rigid.

Preoccupied by her own melancholy thoughts, Gracie did not notice the strangeness of Kate's manner. She took a step forward.

"I'll go up, Aunt Kate. I shan't want any supper."

Kate took a tighter grip of the banister. Her voice, struggling out of the raging tumult of her bosom, sounded smothered.

"No supper! What a pity! Wouldn't you like me to fetch something to your room? Perhaps some chicken and a glass of sherry?"

At first the unaccustomed irony fell short—Gracie gazed at Kate with a vague bewilderment.

"It wouldn't be the slightest trouble, you understand. Why shouldn't you have all your orders? It's a privilege to serve you." Kate was trembling violently now. Unable to maintain her satire any longer, she burst out:

"Where have you been?"

There was a pause. Gracie answered slowly: "I went for a motor run to the loch."

"Who were you with?"

"Frank Harmon. But really, Aunt Kate . . ." There was pain and astonishment in Gracie's voice.

"Don't answer me back," Kate shrilly cut her short. "I've listened to you long enough. You, with your big eyes and your would-be pretty ways. There's not room for both of us in this house any longer. Do you understand what I'm saying to you? Go up to your room tonight with or without your supper. But tomorrow you must find another lodging."

A throbbing silence. Gracie could see Kate's face now, and the sight of it made her pass her hand over her eyes as though to brush away an image that could not be real. Suddenly a thought struck her.

"If you think I'm not giving you enough, I could pay two pounds a week."

Wounded where she was vulnerable, Kate's expression became more bitter.

"So you think it's the money? Well, you're wrong. You might have stayed here for nothing if only you'd behaved yourself. But now . . . now I wouldn't have you if you offered me a fortune."

Gracie's face had hardened. She said rigidly:

"Perhaps you'll tell me what I've done."

It was too much for Kate. Blind with wretchedness and anger, the last of her control broke.

"Done! As if you didn't know. You've brought shame and humiliation on Daniel and me, with your scandalous gallivanting ways. The whole town is talking of you . . . and of us."

For a moment Gracie made no answer. Her face, in the half light, seemed strangely pale. Her eyes, dark and wide in that pale face, were like the eyes of a hurt bird. At last, quietly, she said:

"In that case, Aunt Kate, I'd better leave now."

Without looking at her aunt, who unconsciously made way for her, she went upstairs and along the passage to her room.

With her face still distorted, Kate walked unsteadily into the parlour, where she could hear the sound of drawers being opened and closed on the floor above.

In her heart she felt that her attitude towards Gracie had been unjust and harsh. In a sense she hated herself, and she had to fight down a warm desire to soften, to take Gracie in her arms and tell her that she was sorry, to link up with Daniel and her niece against Susan Mowat's calumnies. But no, because she suffered she had to make others suffer too.

She heard a cab drive up to the gate, heard the cabman enter and help Gracie with her luggage. Then there was silence.

But only for a few moments. Almost at once steps sounded in the hall and Daniel entered the parlour, his face drawn, despondent, and strained by travel.

"Kate," he exclaimed, "who was it that passed me in the street?"

She ground her teeth in impotence. The sight of him, with his woebegone and flustered face, at this crisis, drove her finally to distraction. No matter that she had upheld him to Susan Mowat, no matter that in her heart she loved him. Aloud she shouted:

"It was Gracie Lindsay. A worthless hussy who gets your wife belittled and insulted before the whole town. I've sent her packing."

"No, Kate," he faltered, aghast.

"But I have. And I'd do it again and again to serve you back. When I think on what I've had to put up with I could sink for shame."

She took a sudden step forward and, seizing him by the shoulders, shook him till his teeth rattled. Then suddenly she let him go. Back he went through the open door, staggering giddily until he crashed against the hard oak lintel.

Hysterically, Kate burst into tears, then, turning, fled to her bedroom and closed the door behind her. Her heart was labouring frightfully in her bosom, sending a pain down the inside of her left arm. Why, oh why, did she let herself get upset like this? She wasn't cut out for such scenes, indeed she wasn't. With fingers that trembled she fumbled in the drawer for the heart pills that the doctor had given her and somehow managed to swallow two of them. Then she fell upon her bed and shook with bitter sobs.

Daniel straightened himself up slowly and remained, head clownishly tilted, listening to his wife's smothered weeping upstairs. His rosy mouth was open with a kind of infantile wonder, his clear blue eyes were narrowed by a muddled distress. Kate had never been more incomprehensible to him than at this dreadful moment.

Outside, on the way to the town, Gracie sat in the swaying cab, her burning cheek resting in her palm. The moon, now risen high in the dark, pearly sky, burned with a soft radiance. A tear trickled from beneath Gracie's eyelids and tasted salt in her mouth. Never had she felt so wretched, so desolate and lost. What was her life? How had she deserved this tribulation?

Fifteen minutes later the cab reached the town, drew out of Church Street into College Row, and stopped before Mrs Glen's apartment house, a grey-fronted dwelling rising above its neighbours in the narrow row with an air of dingy respectability.

Here, at No. 3, the widow Glen had earned her livelihood for more than 20 years by taking in lodgers. Apart from her two permanent boarders, the French mistress at the Academy and the librarian of the Institute, Mrs Glen's lodgers were usually young men who did not belong to Levenford, yet came to work, or learn a trade, in the shipyard. Indeed, it was at Glen's that Nisbet Vallance had put up when taking his engineering course at Ralston's eight years before.

But now, perhaps, No. 3 College Row was less superior than it once had been. A general air of seediness hung about the place, and there were those who said that in recent months Margaret Glen had been losing her grip, that lately she had fallen more and more into the weakness which had long afflicted her—an addiction to the bottle.

It was dark when Gracie knocked at the door, and the street lamp opposite threw a pallid light about her.

"Have you a room to let?"

Margaret Glen stood in the doorway, a full-bosomed woman with a very red face and a humid eye. She was dressed in black, her skirt grease-spotted, her blouse gaping where a button was off. She had a warm voice, with an out-of-health catch in it.

"Who are you inquiring for?"

"For myself."

The landlady, making her inspection, peered closer and suddenly let out an exclamation of discovery.

"Goodsakes alive! If it's not Gracie Lindsay! Bless my soul, what fetches you here at this time of night? Are you not staying with your aunt?"

"Not now."

"So that's the way of it." The warm-hearted widow, rendered more sympathetic by her Saturday night potations, nodded her head in complete understanding. "Blood's thicker than water with Kate Nimmo, till it comes to the reckoning. But wait a bit, my dear, Margaret Glen is not like that. No, no. I'll never let it be said that you knocked at *my* door in vain. Your father was a good friend of mine, and Nisbet Vallance too. Come away in. You can have a room and welcome." She raised her voice suddenly to the waiting cabman. "Bring in the gear, Tom. And look sharp if you want a dram."

Thus, despite what Levenford might say, the widow Glen took Gracie in from the simplest motive in the world, an impulse of kindness: while Gracie came to Mrs Glen because she could think of nowhere else to go.

The room towards which the landlady led the way was on the top floor, a high, flower-papered bed-sitting-room at the back of the house.

"Here you are, my dear. And now I'm going to fetch you up some negus. It's turned chilly of a sudden, and you're looking pinched."

The widow retreated and presently returned with a

large steaming glass of hot spirits and water, which Gracie drank gratefully. Then, tired out by the scene with Aunt Kate, perplexed and harassed by the difficulties which had so suddenly come upon her, she washed her hands and face, undressed and slid between the sheets, where the fumes of the grog rising to her head sent her quickly to sleep.

Next morning, after the first surprise of awaking in a strange room had passed, Gracie felt mysteriously tranquil. Of course, she still had troubles, but she felt that they would pass.

Lying on her bed with hands behind her head, she was day-dreaming when the sound of bells reminded her that it was Sunday. A sudden impulse formed in her mind to go to morning service, as she had when she was a girl.

"Ding, dong," went the bells, and the sound uplifted her heart. She felt a poignant desire to face the town, and humbly and bravely to regain the good opinion of those who had condemned her. Rapidly, she got dressed.

Outside it was a brisk morning, and already from all parts of the town a steady stream of decent folks, all solidly conscious of their own worth, moved towards the parish church. The women gloved and bonneted, the men in sober black, all ready to recognise and acknowledge their neighbours according to their station.

"Ding, dong! Ding, dong!" At the corner of Church Street, awaiting her friend Robina Stott, the Provost's wife, and garbed with righteous decorum, stood Miss Paton.

"Good morning." She joined her stately tread with

that of Robina. "There's a fine turnout for the church today! There's the Waldies across the road, with Davie Murray." She bowed low. "Will that be a new suit Murray has on? He cuts a pretty dash for a janitor's son."

"Isabel looks well pleased, at any rate," said the Provost's wife. "She's not a bad figure of a lass."

"She'll be fat like her mother." Miss Paton sniffed. "Mark my words, a house side before she's forty."

"Ding, dong! Ding, dong!" pealed the parish church bells, calling the kindly, the charitable, to prayer. Suddenly Miss Paton let out an exclamation so arresting it drew Robina up.

"Look!" she ejaculated. "For mercy's sake."

There was a pause while the eyes of the two women strained through the gathering worshippers towards a figure emerging from College Row.

"As God is my Maker," said Robina solemnly, "it's Gracie Lindsay!"

Walking alone, Gracie gradually became conscious of the stir she was creating. People looked at her, then looked away. With an outraged air Mrs Waldie drew her daughter more closely to her side. Murray did not seem to see her. Miss Gregg, of the Sewing Guild, indignantly tossed her head.

Gracie coloured, then paled. She had forgotten the power of scandal in a small community, had not dreamed that the town's hostility could be so dark, so bitter, a thing as this. She hesitated, indeed, but it was too late to draw back: mounting the wide stone steps she entered the church.

She went up the aisle, wondering where she should sit, since the place was more crowded than she had expected. Eventually she slipped into one of the side pews not far up, which held only one woman, Miss Isa Dunn.

It was then that the spinster Dunn, hitherto regarded as of no account, wrote her name forever in Levenford history. The moment Gracie entered her pew Miss Dunn drew herself up, lifted her belongings, hymn book, gloves and all, then marched deliberately across the aisle to another pew. A ripple passed over the congregation, silent yet approving.

Gracie sat very still in the deserted pew, a dull pain burning in her heart. She felt that every eye was fixed upon her. She saw that she had made a frightful mistake. She would have given much to be out of the church and back in her room, but now she could not move. With downcast gaze she remained while the church filled up and the minister finally took the pulpit.

The Reverend Douglas Mowat was a great pappy man with rolls of fat behind his collar—indeed, his corpulence had become such a byword in the town that his wife was reported to tie his bootlaces. Certainly he himself could never have reached so far beyond his bulging paunch. "Creishy Mowat" the irreverent named him, though perhaps this was due, in part, to the quality of his sermons, which, particularly when the rich members of his congregation attended at the kirk, were unsurpassable in unctuousness. Creishy had no real goodness, but he had a gift, rare in a taciturn race, of glibness. "When he opens his big blabbing mouth," Apothecary

Hay had sardonically declared, "the words come gushing out like lard from a pig's bladder." In more refined Levenford society the Reverend Douglas was admiringly deemed both "ready" and "eloquent".

Today, indeed, the minister justified this eulogy in full. As he took his stance, heaving his flesh upon the edge of the pulpit, he sensed the tension in the church, and his eye, roving nimbly among his flock, fell upon the intruder—Gracie, alone in the pew.

So tha-at was it! Wha-at an opportunity! Wha-at a chance for drama and a moral! Without scruple or hesitation Mowat abandoned the sermon he had prepared on Isaiah 41 and 6 and, pursing out his big wet lips, declaimed instead:

"Proverbs 7 and 10. 'And behold there came a woman with the attire of an harlot!' "

Dead silence, the bated silence of expectation, then the Reverend Mowat began his sermon. And what a sermon! Even the Provost, who detested Mowat, was forced to admit its power. As for the rest, they swallowed it with rapture.

Creishy had his own reasons, beyond the chance to enhance his oratorical reputation, for the attack. Like most full-bodied men anchored sternly to an unattractive wife, "the bust of the flesh", as he imagined them, invariably unleashed in him a blustering violence.

Besides, he had always nourished a grudge against the Lindsays—old Tom, in the days of the past, had tried hard to get his brother-in-law, Daniel Nimmo, into the pulpit now occupied so worthily by himself. He knew, too, something of the inner situation between his esteemed friends the Waldies and David Murray—there was little that Mowat did not know—and, to cap everything, only the other day the wife of his bosom had come to him with the ominous whisper that she had caught Edward, only son of his loins, "mooning around that Lindsay woman at the Khedive office". Flies and honeypot—yea, verily!

Thus the Reverend Mowat let himself go. He was cautious, mind you, beyond everything Creishy was astute. He had, in his own mind, nothing against Daniel that he would openly declare. Even his strictures against Gracie, if unmistakable, were veiled. He thundered in hyperbole, launched his shafts from Holy Writ itself.

"For the commandment is a lamp to keep thee from the evil woman, from the flattery of the tongue of a strange woman. Lust not after her beauty in thine heart: neither let her take thee with her eyelids. For by means of a whorish woman"—a thrill of suppressed delight ran through the congregation—"a man is brought to a piece of bread".

"Can a man take fire in his bosom and his clothes not be burnt? Can one go upon hot coals and his feet not be burnt? With her much fair speech she caused him to yield, with the flattering of her lips she forced him. He goeth after her straightway, as an ox goeth to the slaughter or as a fool to the correction of the stocks. Hearken unto me now therefore and attend to the words of my mouth. Her house is the way to hell, going down to the chambers of death!"

Seated there among them, Gracie heard it all. At first she scarcely understood. And then she saw it was for her, each word a stone hurled at her head. She could not move. There was something frightening in her immobility, for chaos was within her, and such a revulsion of feeling as was almost insupportable. She had come here to pray, to find tolerance and understanding. And this was what they did to her.

It was over at last. With a sigh of repletion the congregation got up and the church began to empty. Had Gracie been wise she would have risen at once. As it was she remained a few moments, trying to collect her scattered forces, forgetful that outside the people would collect to gossip and exchange their views upon the minister's achievement of the day. Thus, when she did take her leave she was forced to confront them all, more intimately, more cruelly than before.

Down the steps she came, between the various groups. She came slowly, hoping to find one friendly face, someone with whom she might exchange a single word of greeting. But there was no one. The conversation died as she went past. Heads were turned away. Not one soul came forward to acknowledge her. A little choking sob rose in Gracie's throat. With her head down, she turned and went back to her lodging.

That afternoon the sun came out, melting the grey clouds and intensifying the stillness of the holy day. In her room, seated in the wicker chair, Gracie stared unseeingly at the drab vista of chimney pots before her.

If only Frank Harmon had been in town he, at least, would have proved a standby, a distraction, but he had gone to London for a week on business. When darkness fell she was still there, nor did she stir until Mrs Glen, in some concern, toiled up the stairs and knocked upon the door to inquire solicitously what ailed her.

"This'll never do at all." The landlady entered, her face slightly flushed, her breath heavy with the smell of spirits. "I cannot bear to see you sitting alone. Come away down to my fireside."

Gracie shook her head.

"I'd be poor company for you, Mrs Glen."

"Tut, tut, my dear, I'll not take no. Never mind what they say about you. I'll give you a drop that'll cheer you up."

For an instant Gracie hesitated, then she stood up. After all, why should she not accept this kindly hospitality? A drink would do her good. What did she care? If the saints of the town had disowned her, then she must consort with sinners. She submitted as Mrs Glen slipped an arm about her waist and escorted her downstairs.

Chapter IV

IN THE SUMMER months Daniel enjoyed the early morning more than any other part of the day. He rose at six, and when he had taken Kate her cup of tea, moving silently in his old carpet slippers about the quiet, blind-drawn house, he would slip into his garden, his trousers braced over his nightshirt, with an old brown working jacket buttoned across his spare chest, and there he would savour the dew-drenched sweetness of the dawn.

As the long veils of vapour melted from the Winton hills before the yellow sun, and the still beauty of the summer landscape swam to reality through the mist, Daniel worked in his garden. The cows from Drummers Farm, new milked, streamed into the fields, lowing gently. Great beads of dew winked and gleamed in the calceolaria flowers. And Daniel, his heart overflowing, felt the imprint of the Creator's hand fresh upon the earth.

But on this Monday morning, a week after Gracie's departure from his house, Daniel's heart was troubled. His garden had never looked better. His sweet peas were giant high, a glorious line of white, pink and mauve—four, five, even six blooms to a stem, with budding shoots holding promise of more splendid things to come.

Yet Daniel's gaze was absent, his mind apprehensive and disturbed. The objective upon which he had set his heart, which now more than ever had become vital and immediate, seemed no nearer his attainment.

All through these past weeks he had explored every avenue in his search for Gracie's child, his quest for information as to the present whereabouts of the woman Lang. And all in vain. Again and again, on some illusory clue, he had journeyed to neighbouring towns and cities, only to have his hopes dashed rudely to the ground.

In a despondent frame of mind he re-entered the house, took his breakfast, and set out for work. He was a trifle behind his usual time, for the town clock struck half-past eight as he passed the Cross. Instinctively he hastened his pace. And then, as he turned Hay's corner, the postman, already on his forenoon round, stopped him and handed him a letter. It was an official-looking letter, the envelope blue in colour, and with a queer pricking of his skin Daniel opened it.

County Court,
Winton,
July 29th, 1911.

Dear Sir,

With regard to your inquiry of the 7th ult., we have lately had access to the files of the City Court and are now in a position to advise you that Mrs Annie Lang, late of Methven, Perthshire, is at present residing at 17, Clyde Place, Kirkbridge. Recently Mrs Lang appeared before the lower court on a charge of contravening Statute 15a of the Child Welfare Act and was placed on probation by the S.P.C.C.

If we can be of further service to you in this matter do not hesitate to get in touch with us.

I am, sir, your obedient servant,

Andrew Ross.

Clerk to the Winton Sessions.

A stifled cry broke from Daniel, a cry of joy and triumph. At last, at last, he was on the right track. Despite the faintly disquieting tone of the letter, the news which it contained was positive and official. After all his fruitless forays he greeted it like a shining beacon in a dark and stormy sea. There was not a moment to be lost. He would not open the studio today. Suffused by a new confidence, a new strength, he looked at his watch, and without hesitation swung round and started towards the railway station.

Here, after only a short wait, he took his place in a third-class compartment of the nine o'clock train for Winton. As the engine laboured through the low-lying country of the valley he sat tense and eager, his eyes directed unseeingly towards the rush-fringed marshland where a few cattle browsed stolidly in the drizzling rain.

He reached Kirkbridge after noon, when the cotton-thread mills which constituted the main industry of this large industrial outpost of the city of Winton were disgorging their workers for the dinner-break. Hundreds of women, with shawls over their heads, streamed through the big gates like an army on the march. Over this sombre scene the rain fell steadily from a leaden sky, turning the cobbled road into a sea of mud.

Daniel asked a policeman the way to Clyde Place and, turning up his collar, plunged into the crowd. At the end of the main street he turned left and, passing an iron statue of one of the great mill-owners of the district, he entered a poorer part of the town.

Daniel had never before seen such dreary shops. The gutters ran with evil-smelling liquid, the effluent from the dye-works. In the courts grubby washing hung from the lines. Almost every doorway led to a bar, or to a bookmaker's office.

Daniel's worst fears were realised. Mrs Lang, the guardian of Gracie's son, had fallen even lower than he had already feared.

Crossing a cobbled square he entered a narrow street, like a canal between the high buildings. This gutter, running with stinking mud, carried a chipped blue enamel plaque—Clyde Place.

Daniel was taken by a sinking weariness, physical and spiritual. The smell, the stench of the alley, the slum dwellings which rose on each side, turned him cold.

It was so dark, too, that even on the brightest day few gleams of sun could ever penetrate. It was like the bottom of a well. It made Daniel want to slink away, to fly to some wide open heath and there to purify his being with the country air.

But Daniel's nervous excitement, now amounting almost to hysteria, would not let him draw back. He entered the passage leading to No. 17 and began to mount the stairs. The stair was no worse than was ordinary in that district—since the tenement was built on the back-to-back principle, there were no windows, light or air. The gas brackets were plugged, and a cracked pipe had stained one landing.

Up three flights Daniel went, gathering his resources in a breathless prayer, when suddenly he stumbled and almost fell. A child was sitting upon the stairs, a boy. Daniel stared at him through the fog-like gloom. He seemed to be passing the time in a philosophical fashion, by playing with some small round stones which he tossed in the air and caught on the back of his hand.

But Daniel hardly noticed that. It was the boy himself that held his startled eye. Daniel knew about rickets, knew also that rickets in those slum places, from poor diet and lack of sunlight, was a prevailing sickness. And now he saw quite plainly how this child's legs were curled under him and how small he was, how his head seemed too heavy for him to hold up. He held it with one hand, bracing his elbow against his knee. His eyes were dark and serious in his pinched face. His skin was the colour of tallow, dull and without lustre. He didn't seem to wear many clothes—just bits and pieces of garments that had been made down for him. He might have been seven years of age.

Sitting there, he took Daniel in with his grave, rather tired eyes. Then Daniel found his tongue.

"Does Mrs Lang live here?"

After a pause the boy nodded, seriously.

"I'd like to see her," Daniel said.

"Is it the rent you're after?" asked the little boy. "I'm afraid she cannot pay you."

"I don't want to be paid. I only want to speak to her."

The child hesitated, considering Daniel in his own attentive fashion. Then he said slowly:

"All right. I'll show you."

He got up. He did this like all rickety children, holding on to his legs and struggling clumsily to an erect position. It was difficult. But at last it was done and, limping, he led the way upstairs.

On the top landing he stopped before a door. From the boy's manner Daniel saw it was his own door. Then, as he swung round and looked up, the light from the broken skylight fell upon him.

For the first time Daniel really saw the child's face. He gave a stifled exclamation and a heavy wave of emotion broke over him—he felt it strike him as a ship might feel the buffeting of a heavy wave. That upturned face, although so frail and pallid, was unmistakable in its likeness to Gracie's face.

Foreshortened, caught by the grey light, the face emerged from its drab background and seemed to swim with a quality luminous and visionary, as though Gracie herself were hazily evoked before him. The eyes especially, those wide hazel eyes, so gravely fixed upon him, could never be denied. Daniel swallowed dumbly. Indistinctly he said:

"What is your name?"

The boy answered: "I'm called Robert."

"But your other name?" In his emotion, Daniel was

speaking brusquely. "Is it Lang? Is Mrs Lang your mother?"

"Yes, Annie Lang's my mother," Robert said vaguely. "Anyhow, I stop with her." As though unwilling to be questioned more, he pushed the door open, the door of his house.

It was a single room. At the end of the room a woman sat cross-legged on a flock mattress stretched on the bare linoleum. She was stitching rapidly some cloth which lay in her lap, her needle flying with a deadly, automatic monotony.

Even in the turmoil of his mind Daniel took in the poor furnishings of the apartment, the rusted stove, cracked china and torn blinds.

In the near corner three children, all younger than Robert, were playing with the lid of an old tin can. Beside the mattress lay a pile of half-finished coarse serge trousers.

Robert went over to the woman: then, with the carefulness which marked all his actions, he moved his eyes towards Daniel and murmured in her ear.

Mrs Lang bit off a length of black cotton from her reel, glancing first at Robert, then at Daniel.

"Can folks not let us be?" she complained. "What harm have I done?"

"It's not that," Robert pacified her. "The man just wants to talk to you."

Before she could answer he turned, rounded up the playing children and packed them through the door. As he limped after them he turned to Daniel with a grave air of achievement, and nodded as if implying that he might now proceed in private with his business. There was something in that gesture, so wistful, yet so wise, which made Daniel's eyes smart. But the woman's voice broke in on him.

"What is it you want? You see I'm busy. I must finish this work by seven."

Daniel fastened his earnest gaze on Annie Lang. She was a poor raddled creature, not old, yet worn out, it seemed, by ill-living and adversity. On each of her cheeks was a hard flush and beneath her eyes were tiny bluish pouches. Her ankles, visible beneath the hem of her tattered skirt, were swollen and shapeless. She sat with a shawl pulled about her shoulders. Not for a second had she stopped stitching since he entered the room.

Daniel cleared his throat, swallowed convulsively.

"I came about that boy," he said. "The boy you call Robert."

There was a pause. She did not speak, made no effort to help him. It was not easy for him to continue with her furtive glances darting towards him. Yet somehow he went on, making plain why he had come and what he wished of her.

At first her expression remained dull and fretful, but as he proceeded it altered, revealing in turn emotions which she tried clumsily to hide—surprise, slow comprehension, then a quick and calculating shiftiness. She stopped sewing, letting her work fall into her lap, braced herself to meet Daniel's eyes.

"Well," she said at last, "I'll not deny he's the boy you are seeking. He's the Lindsay child right enough."

He had not doubted that: he had known it five minutes ago on the landing. He pressed on eagerly, hurriedly:

"Then let me take him away with me. I'll take him back today."

She shook her head decisively and answered, speaking rapidly:

"No, no! I couldn't do it. I couldn't even think of it. The child was made over to me. I have the papers to prove it. And I couldn't do without him. He helps me in a heap of different ways. He goes all over the place for my messages. You can see for yourself how wise he is. I'm not strong now, you know. I've had a hard time of it since my husband died. Ever since we left the farm it's been a struggle to keep alive. Besides, I'm fond of Robert. He's a good little thing. And the money I've spent on him, with him being delicate and needing physic in the winter—ay, ay, I've got to take that into consideration. You'll understand, of course, that when the old man Lindsay passed away there was never another penny of help for me."

She broke off as though she had said enough, and began, with contracted lips, to sew again. Yet Daniel, for all his simpleness, had read her face. He did not hesitate.

"How much do you want? I'll pay you if you let me have the boy."

She dropped her sewing again, her veined hands, the fingers blue-stippled by innumerable needle pricks, clutching nervously at her shawl. Though she made an effort to conceal it, his words agitated her profoundly.

For her piecework sewing, her sole support in these past two years, she received on an average 1s. 3d. a day, out of which she was obliged to purchase cotton and sometimes buttons. But now, by a stroke of fortune, had come this opportunity. Fearful of demanding too much, yet desperately afraid of not asking enough, she hovered in a pitiable indecision.

"Would you—would you go to the length of £20?"

Daniel gazed at her, as much distressed as she—he knew nothing of the legal processes involved or of the validity of her claim upon the child. It never struck him that the threat of prosecution on the grounds of neglect would have quickly made her change her attitude. His nature was too mild for such a stratagem. And he wanted Robert. One look at that meagre face, at that crippled figure, had hardened his intention, driven him to most abandoned recklessness. The child must come out of here, if it cost him everything he had. He took a leap in the dark.

"I'll give you £20. I haven't got it now. But I'll bring it to you—" He thought rapidly. "The day after tomorrow. And then I'll take the boy back to his mother."

She stared at him, as in a trance. It was unbelievable, he was going to give her £20. Dear God! What could she not do with that—£20! It would make a new woman of her, bring her comfort and relief from drudgery, oh, it would last for ever. Suddenly, without warning, she burst into tears.

"Oh, dearie me," she snivelled. "I don't know what you'll think of me. It's like I was selling you the boy. But as God's my judge I wouldn't do it if I didn't need the money. You've no idea what it is to be poor and helpless, and to have come down in the world."

Daniel allowed her to exhaust her tears. Then, as she dried her eyes with the edge of her shawl, he said in a tone which he tried to keep from trembling:

"Will we have the boy in now? . . . Just so I can see him again?"

Daniel reached Levenford at eight o'clock that evening in a state of great elation. As the train swung round the curve of Dumbreck the last blink of the sunset caught him—it had cleared in the late afternoon to an unexpected brightness—and he felt as if he were travelling on buoyant waves of light.

His clothes had dried on him during the homeward journey, making his chest tight and his limbs stiff. There was a singing in his ears as he hastened along Church Street, in the gloaming, towards Gracie's lodging. But Daniel did not mind. And although he had eaten scarcely anything all day long he did not dream of going home for supper until he had seen Gracie. He must tell her the great news at once.

But, alas! for his eagerness—Gracie was not at home. When he knocked at No. 3 College Row Mrs Glen came to the door, and, glancing over the top of his head, answered cautiously:

"She left the house at six o'clock."

Daniel's face fell.

"When will she be back?"

"Well," the landlady spoke with due discretion, "she didn't mention when she'd be in. I shouldn't think that she'd be late. Though, mind you, I wouldn't like to say for certain."

Daniel still lingered.

"You don't know where she's gone?"

"I haven't the least idea." After a momentary hesitation the landlady gave him her evasive, professional smile. "I'm not one for inquiring where my boarders are going. That would never do at all, at all. What an awful day it's been, though to be sure it's finer now. Maybe we'll get it warm again tomorrow. Good-night to you, Mr Nimmo, and safe home."

With the door shut gently in his face Daniel had no alternative but to turn away. Yet he could not retreat tamely to the toll road. He must talk to someone. He must, he must. The thrilling news of his discovery, of all that he had done and now proposed to do, was more than his breast could humanly contain. The streets were quite dark now, the shops had closed a good half-hour ago. And so he set off to call upon his friend the druggist.

Hay, at least, was not from home. He sat in his room above the shop with carpet slippers on his large feet and Mill's Logic on his bony knees. Detached from his counter and at ease, he assumed even more completely an air of omniscient cynicism.

When Daniel appeared the druggist gazed at him—that ironic scrutiny which Hay termed "giving him a look". Then, before Daniel could speak, he remarked satirically:

"So it's you yourself, my bonny wee man! Come in.

But don't trip over yourself. By the law of gravity, you're liable to fall down."

Daniel was too elevated to be annoyed. He took a chair and exultantly exclaimed:

"I've found him!"

The druggist studied Daniel across his long nose.

"I guessed as much. Man, you're the perfect example of *homo eedioticus.* Haven't you got into enough trouble over that woman without bothering about her brat?"

"You mustn't talk that way," Daniel protested warmly. "I tell you, Apothecary, he's made a powerful impression on me, this child. He's only a little scrap of a thing. And the place he lives in—it's just a sink of corruption. I don't believe he's ever seen a green field or had a breath of pure air in all his life. And yet he never as much as lets out a whimper. It's, oh man, it's an inspiration."

Hay laughed his most aggravating laugh.

"What kind of twaddle is this you're giving me?"

"It's gospel truth." Daniel was not to be put down. "He's an extraordinary boy. Seven years old and he faces up to things like a man. You ought to see the way he looks after the woman Lang—she's been poorly lately—and the other children too. He ought to have a better chance. He should have had it long ago. We've got to get him out of that place. It is his only chance."

"Go on with you! And when you have got him, what will you do with him?"

"Don't you understand that the mother as well as the son will gain from this? Gracie will make him a home. You may laugh, but that will be the saving of her. I will find her a place a little way from Levenford, where everyone has been so unkind to her."

He paused to regain his breath, and then continued: "I tell you, my friend, that, God willing, I will have brought mother and son together before the end of the week."

"Those are your plans," said the druggist pityingly. "Have you thought what plans the excellent young woman may have?"

"I am going to look for her. She has gone out."

"Is that so? What an extraordinary coincidence! Where is she?"

"How should I know?" retorted Daniel, reddening.

"Obviously. How should you know?" Hay laughed loudly. "You never said a truer word in your life. How . . . ha! ha! . . . how should you know?"

Daniel looked puzzled.

"My poor friend," resumed the druggist scornfully. "You really are a sad idiot! You have such a way of arranging things! Imagine the hornets' nest you will stir up, the scandal you will provoke in the good town of Levenford which is still resounding to the name of Gracie Lindsay. And you propose to bring her bastard here in front of everyone? Do you want to have the whole town on your heels and on Gracie's?"

Daniel pressed his lips obstinately.

"I can't leave him in that slum any longer. What else can I do?"

There was a silence. The druggist lay back in his

chair inspecting the heel of his carpet slipper, which was almost falling off, with the conscious air of a man of affairs.

"Well, I'll tell you what you could do," said he at length, drawing down the corners of his mouth. "Mind you, I haven't a brass farthing's worth of interest in your Gracie Lindsay or her—well—what I said before. But Heavens, I just hate to see you make a fool of yourself, ay, and maybe worse, for there's folks in this town, Mowat, Waldie and a few others, who would put their knife into you, deep, deep, over this business." He smiled scornfully. "Because of that, I'm half inclined to lend you a hand."

There was a dramatic pause. Then, fortifying himself with a nugget of liquorice, Hay resumed.

"Maybe you'll mind my houseboat on the loch, that's to say if you have any mind at all. Well! This boy is half dead, according to your own statement, dyin' for a breath of fresh air. As for his bonny mother, the sooner she's out of this royal borough of Levenford the healthier for her and all concerned. If you knew a certain Mr Harmon as well as me, you might grasp the full significance of that remark. So I'll tell you what I'll do for you, my daft little man, I'll give you my houseboat for the boy and Gracie, and they can have a holiday together there till they're ready to go to the grand new place you're finding for them."

A little gasp broke from Daniel's lips as the full worth of the idea dawned upon him. It was quite true what Hay said, he himself was a muddler, he had no head for detail or arrangement. He had worried himself to death over the complications of the situation, yet he could never have conceived an expedient so brilliant, so simple as this. Why, it solved the whole difficulty at once.

"Man," he stammered, between admiration and gratitude. "It's a master-stroke."

Hay waved Daniel's thanks away with the air of one superior to all the pettifogging emotions of humanity. Nevertheless he condescended, indeed he seemed anxious in a lordly fashion, to expound the merits of his own invention.

Thus, half an hour later, when Daniel took his leave, the thing lay plain between them. The Lord doth move in mysterious ways His wonders to perform. Who, thought Daniel, would dare to question the hand of Providence at such a moment and on such a night? Tears came to his eyes as he marched along.

And then, as he reached the end of College Road, he saw a woman turn the corner in front of him and mount the steps of No. 3. It was Gracie. Suppressing an impulse to call out, Daniel hurried after her, reaching the entrance as she was about to close the front door.

"Daniel!" she exclaimed, recognising him with a start. She pressed her side uncertainly, her key still in her hand. "What a fright you gave me! Why are you out at this time of night?"

"Why are you, Gracie?" he asked, an imperceptible doubt in his tone.

"Me?" she uttered the word as though discarding it. "I've been to an entertainment."

"With whom, Gracie?"

"Oh, with my friend and employer, Frank Harmon." She smiled with that new faint note of bitterness. Her cheeks were a trifle flushed, her eyes seemed unnaturally bright. Then, catching sight of his face, she relented suddenly, bending forward with a warm impulsiveness. "There, there! Do not look so doleful, you poor little man. There's nothing between Frank and me. We only went to the concert at Overton's, if you want to know. I cannot sit alone twiddling my thumbs all the evening. Can I now?"

For some reason he was conscious of a queer dismay. He had never seen her so brittle, so unlike herself. The lightness of her tone rang completely false. She seemed in some strange way to mock herself.

"Don't stare at me so hard, Daniel dear. You make me feel quite giddy. But what am I doing keeping you standing here in the cold? Come away in. We'll call up Mrs Glen. She'll give us a glass of negus in her snug back-parlour."

Her manner was so odd, so overwrought, it quite alarmed him, as also did the suspicious odour of her breath. He followed her into the passage, but stopped at the foot of the staircase where a gas jet, coldly moping in a yellow globe, cast a wavering light upon them.

"Wait, Gracie," he whispered nervously. "I'll go no farther. I only wanted you to know that I went to Kirkbridge today." He drew a deep breath. "I've—I've found the boy."

There was a sudden silence, filled only by the faint splutter of the gas jet.

"Yes, my dear," he nodded. "You can have him back now any time you choose."

She turned slowly, steadying herself against the wall. Her expression, caught between that high, unreal gaiety and the sudden comprehension of his words, wore an arrested, a rigid look. Her hand was drawn back as if he had suddenly flashed a bright light upon her face.

"What did you say?" she murmured indistinctly.

He repeated what he had already said.

"So that's it." She rubbed her forehead slowly with her hand as though trying to erase disconnecting and confusing thoughts. "Tell me—tell me how you found him."

Standing there in the lobby of the lodging-house he told her what he had done and what, with Hay's help, he proposed to do.

When he had finished she gazed at him, her lower lip drooping moistly, her eyes so dark in her pale face their pupils seemed to have overflowed.

"What kind of woman am I?" She spoke in a distraught and helpless tone. "I don't know. I wish somebody would tell me."

Then suddenly she leaned against the wall, buried her face in her arms, and began to cry. She cried silently, yet with such abandon that at last Daniel touched her arm in timid protest.

"Just let me cry," she sobbed. "I feel I could never

cry enough. And, oh dear, oh dear, I have an awful headache."

"Don't take it so hard, Gracie," he whispered, upset. "It's not easy for you now. But you'll find that it'll all come right in the end."

She stopped weeping at last. As she dried her eyes a dry, nervous spasm, a kind of shudder, shook her body. She faced him humbly.

"I'm sorry, Uncle Daniel. I'll not be this way again." Again that spasm, suppressed, almost hysterical. "I've a feeling the concert didn't agree with me." She raised her head slowly. "I must go up, I suppose. Thank you for all you've done for me. I'll not stop any longer now. Somehow I'm half-dead with sleep."

She gave him a wan smile, travesty of the joyous gratitude he had expected, and began, quite unsteadily, to mount the stairs. He gazed after her, standing there a minute after she had gone from sight, smoothing his little beard with a puzzled, deprecating, troubled gesture.

Gracie was strange tonight, yes, even before he had told her she had acted queerly. With a sense of vague distress he turned and quietly left the house, setting his steps towards home.

Across the Common his feet dragged upon the incline and his legs were stiff and weary. He became aware of himself as a sorely tired man with a sharp pain in his side. There might be difficulties with Kate, too, a demand for an explanation of his lateness he could not give.

Yet the thought of all that the day had brought was warm within him, a sense of accomplishment, of thanksgiving. And the dearest thought of all was that grave, that pallid little face as he had first seen it emerging from the shadow of the squalid staircase in Clyde Place.

Chapter V

THE FOLLOWING NIGHT David Murray, bridegroom-elect and rising young man of Levenford, sat at his supper with a set and brooding frown. Hovering about in the shadows of the clean, bare living-room, with its spotless hearth and shining fender, its varnished wallpaper and brass weighted clock, his mother studied him.

"You'll have another cup, Davie dear?"

At first he hardly seemed to hear her, then with a start he lifted his head.

"No, no, mother. I can barely finish this one." He stirred his cocoa and made pretence of drinking it.

She gazed at him solicitously. All her life she had worked for him, denied herself food and clothing, forgone everything in order that he might have what was good for him—as a boy, as a growing lad, as a student, poring late over his books in this same room.

Now that he was successful she still clung to her habits of self-denial and effacement. Despite his remonstrances she would not even sit at table with him, but served him hand and foot throughout the meal.

Her joy lay not in what he could give her but in the treasured thought that she had helped to make him what he was. Every upward step which he had taken brought her a deeper satisfaction. The esteem in which he was held was sweeter to her than manna from heaven.

And now his marriage with Isabel Waldie, daughter of the richest, the most important man in Levenford—it would be the crowning glory of his career! Often, often, in these last few days, moving about the old-fashioned and rather ill-lit house that stood tucked away at the back of Skinners Wynd, she had raised her eyes and thought: "Oh! If his father could only see him now!"

Tonight, however, she sensed that he was not his usual self and a worried line drew between her brows. She did not dream of presuming to question him direct, yet when she had silently removed his cup, as if in the hope that he might speak, she murmured:

"You've had a hard day of it, son?"

He nodded absently. The Town Council's monthly meeting had taken place that afternoon and settled the final plans for the new gasworks scheme. He had been complimented on his purchase of the Langloan property, then afterwards, as the Council members sat relaxed, with the customary refreshment of whisky before them, the Provost had jovially raised his glass.

"Gentlemen, there's going to be a wedding soon . . . I'd like to propose the health of our friend David and his future bride, Miss Waldie."

Recollection of that final toast made Murray wince. His silence increased his mother's anxiety. Seeing that he would eat no more, she began disconsolately to gather up the dishes.

"You'll be for Knoxhill tonight?"

"Not tonight," he replied heavily. "I saw Waldie at the meeting. The house is full of dressmakers."

"Then I'll make up the fire for you," she said quickly. "It's turned chilly of a sudden."

He rose abruptly.

"No! I think I'll take a walk tonight, mother."

"A walk!" Her eyes fluttered towards him with renewed anxiety. In his student days he had often taken long, solitary walks at night to clear his tired brain. But now, this was different, and strangely disturbing.

She watched him go into the little lobby, pull on his cloth cap, and take his stick from the cupboard under the stairs. Hardly aware of what she did, she followed him into the hall, her gaze imploring, her hand clutching the sleeve of his coat.

"Promise me—promise me you'll not do anything foolish, Davie!"

He looked down at her, and his laugh was savage in her ears.

"Have I ever done anything foolish in all my life? Don't fret yourself, mother. I'm the model son, the model citizen, the model husband-to-be. I couldn't be anything else if I tried, God pity me!"

And with that she had to be content, standing long in the doorway, watching his swinging figure disappear into the darkness of the Wynd, in the direction of Church Street.

Up the length of Church Street Murray went, then back again at the same violent pace, his head down, his blank pipe between his teeth, like a man driven to furious movement by some torturing indecision in his blood.

Suddenly he broke to the right and entered College Row. Opposite No. 3, but on the other side of the Row, he drew up. It was quite dark in the narrow passage, for the street lamps at the end threw but a blur of shadows. Pressed back against an archway Davie let his eyes fall feverishly upon the lodging-house of Margaret Glen. Should he go in or should he not?

Before he could make up his mind he became conscious of a waft of cigarette smoke travelling towards him, and a moment later he discerned someone in a light dustcoat, high collar and soft hat pacing the pavement with a slow but gallant tread. In a flash Davie recognised the weedy elegant—it was Edward Mowat, the minister's son—and his gorge rose at the sight. He stepped out across the path of the troubadour.

"Why, hello, Murray!" exclaimed the bold Edward. "What are you doing here?"

"That's precisely what I want to ask you."

Creishy's son sniggered. He was a long link of a youth, with a slack mouth, a watery eye, and a doggy air of knowing his way about. A student at the University of Winton, he stood in his own and his parents' eyes as a paragon of wit and manliness.

"Might ask you the same question, old man. Haw, haw! Woman, lovely woman, eh? Takes a college man to appreciate the form divine. Never know your luck on a night like this. Haw, haw! Have a cigarette. Shall we join forces and hunt together?"

Murray breathed hard. Has it come to this, he

thought, that the half-baked whelps of the town were hanging around her? He took young Mowat by the collar.

"Get out of here," he hissed. "If you're not away in ten seconds, I'll haul you straight home to your reverend father and tell him where I found you."

"Oh! I say," Edward flustered. "Look here now—"

"Quick!" said Murray. "You've got five seconds left!"

Don Juan flung a pale glance at David, then with a scared, "What about yourself?" slunk hurriedly away.

Murray moistened his lips as though to remove a bad and bitter taste. At least he had saved her from that indignity.

He took up his vigil again and soon his heart beat violently. The door of No. 3 opened and Gracie came out, without a hat and with a coat thrown over her shoulders.

She hesitated, and it was obvious that she was worried. Since Daniel's visit she had thought of nothing but her son, the child she had abandoned so many years before. These strange feelings, she told herself, were not affection but a mixture of anxiety and fear—yes, fear of the responsibility that her uncle wanted her to assume, and to which she did not feel equal. Could she start her life again on this new basis? She did not know. She dreaded this new experience.

Invisible in the shadows, David watched her stop at the foot of the steps, as though to enjoy the freshness of the evening air. Then she moved on. After a brief struggle he came to a decision. He followed Gracie.

She walked slowly but without hesitation, as if towards a definite destination. When she reached the outskirts of the town, at the corner of the old road to Garshake, she paused under the last lamp-post. Before he had time to think, David joined her.

"Gracie!"

She turned, and her eyes shone in the pale light of the street-lamp. She was silent. Perhaps she was moved? He could not be sure. When she spoke her voice was calm and firm.

"Well, here is our dear Davie Murray! The Count Murray himself!"

"Make mock of me, if you wish. I daresay I deserve it all. But Gracie!" Murray's tone suddenly was urgent. "I must talk to you."

"The Earl wants to talk," she reasoned, with deeper irony. "But it's too late for talking now, surely. Besides, I have an appointment with a gentleman. I'm waiting on him now."

"You don't mean Harmon?"

"Why not?" Gracie answered carelessly.

The truth was that she had half promised to join the agent for a short walk that evening but, in her stress of mind, had felt herself quite unable to fulfil the engagement. She had come, actually, to their meeting place for the purpose of conveying to him this decision. But now, before David, she chose to ignore this, and to magnify the significance of the occasion.

Murray ground his teeth together.

"He's a bad lot, Gracie . . . selfish and ruthless under that smooth manner . . . and so inordinately vain. He's had other affairs with women here. And they haven't ended very nicely. Harmon is too dangerous to fool around with. He isn't to be trusted. For all his posing as a gay bachelor, he has a wife somewhere, in England. He's a married man."

"And you soon will be, David."

"For heaven's sake, Gracie, don't be so hard on me. I know I've got myself tangled up. But I'm—I'm fond of you, woman. And it drives me crazy to see you in a pass like this, with the whole town talking about you, Gracie! Let's go somewhere and try to straighten things out for you."

"Haven't I told you I can't?" She paused, struck by a thought which made her sad eyes flash with bitter mockery. "Unless you would like to come with us . . . if you're not afraid of Frank!"

He flushed again.

"I'm only afraid for you."

She seemed to smile into herself, her eyes travelling beyond him, as footsteps sounded on the pavement. It was, in fact, Harmon who approached them.

"Good evening, Frank," Gracie greeted him with that same pretended gaiety. "Now, don't scowl like that. You must behave yourself. It seems we're to have company tonight. The Earl of Murray is coming with us for a stroll."

Harmon was plainly put out by Murray's unexpected presence and by Gracie's dark and reckless mood.

"Hasn't he something better to do?" he asked pointedly.

"Oh dear, oh dear!" Gracie exclaimed, in assumed

rebuke. "Where are your manners, Frank? The Earl's not used to such rough talk. If you're not more careful he'll run home to his mother."

In spite of his suspicions, a slow smile broke over Harmon's face.

"Let him come if he wants," he declared indifferently. "Where shall we go?"

"To Ladywell, Frank. That's the place for select company."

Frank merely shrugged his shoulders and they began to move along the Garshake road, Harmon taking one side of Gracie and Murray, in a kind of dogged fury, the other. Now that he had gone so far, David would not turn back. The thought of Gracie meeting Harmon here and walking out with him to Ladywell rankled like wormwood in his breast.

"Now, don't look so upset," Gracie spoke with ironic solicitude. "I know it's not what you're accustomed to, but it's the only place about here. And what can't be cured must be endured."

The inn, indeed, was small and primitive, no more than a long, low room with a bar at one end and a fireplace, wherein smouldered a log of green wood, at the other. Two tables were spaced on the wooden floor, and from the smoky ceiling there hung an oil swing-lamp with a cracked and sooty chimney. At present the place was empty.

There was a moment's pause after they entered, then the door behind the bar creaked open and a tall, raw-boned woman emerged, holding her knitting in one hand. She was a gaunt creature, the landlady, with harsh features and an inflammation of her eyelids. Shading her gaze against the lamplight, she peered at Gracie and her face drew into a sycophantic smile.

"It's yourself, my dearie, with your fine, free-handed friend: and another gentleman besides." Advancing, she dusted a corner of one table with her sleeve. "What'll you have?"

"I'll take whisky," Harmon said shortly.

"And what's the Earl's will?" Gracie inquired.

"I'll have whisky, too," Davie said angrily.

"And I'll have my usual glass of port." She seated herself at the table between Harmon and Murray with a sigh of feigned contentment.

Murray took up his whisky, his eyes fixed on Gracie, a dark flush still burning on his brow. Never, never had he known her like this, so wild and wanton, so mingling laughter with dark bitterness, and through it all masking with unconcern a sadness so unbearable it seemed about to break her heart.

He loved and pitied her, at once. And all the puritan in him recoiled against her presence here in such a mood, at such a questionable hour. Though he said nothing, she must have read this in his face. For her glance met his and mocked it.

"Are you at your devotions, Davie, dear? You've such a look of piety. I believe you'd like to get us started on a psalm tune. Or would it be the wedding march? Out of respect to dear Miss Waldie and the elect of Levenford."

Harmon, helping himself to more whisky, laughed shortly, enjoying the mortification which flooded

Murray's face. Gracie's eyes flashed. The raw wine now was singing in her head.

"You may well laugh, Frank." Her voice shook unexpectedly. "It's the only thing to do. Poor Uncle Dan, with his 'love one another and be kind!' Hate one another, under the veil of godliness—that's the watchword in this town. And if some poor wretch gets out of step in the church parade, then heaven help him or her."

With a passionate gesture she drank her wine, then stared remotely at the empty glass. Her tone turned softer. "When I came back to Levenford my heart was filled with joy. I loved the place, I felt it was my own, that I was home again. And what has happened to me?" Her eyes filled up with tears. "But I'm not caring. Since they don't want me here, I'll go away. Yes, away, David Murray, if it's any comfort for you to know it. Uncle Dan has arranged it, and he's the best man among you . . . I'm going. . . ."

Here she broke off with something very near a sob, checking her impulse to reveal the full prospect which lay ahead for her and which, through all this evening, had lain oppressively upon her heart.

"Listen," Gracie said, "and I'll sing you a song. It's the sweetest of them all, about a lass named Annie Laurie, who might just as well have been me."

Rising to her feet, she faced them giddily. The smoky lamp made shadows all around her and the scent of burning wood had filled her hair. Her voice came sweet and true, with a wild yet tender quality which would have melted any heart.

Murray's spirit groaned within him. Even Harmon seemed, in some way, moved. His eyes travelled over Gracie with heavy appreciation, a sudden intensification of his possessiveness. And when the song was ended he stood up.

"That was fine, Gracie . . . too good for this den. Let's get out of it." He took her arm. "You can sing some more in my rooms."

Murray could hold himself in check no longer. All at once he forgot discretion, his position, and the circumstances of his life. He jumped up with a nervous violence that sent his chair clattering behind him.

"Let her be," he said in a choking voice. "It's time she went home."

Still with Gracie's arm in his, Harmon gave Murray a sultry look. "Are you addressing me?"

"I'm telling you to leave her alone."

"Or what?" said Harmon, without moving a muscle.

Gracie clapped her hands with a wild exclamation. David's face was white as paper. Within him, his tortured sensibilities writhed like serpents, but the whisky he had drunk made him dead outside, like a man coated with rubber. He had no fear. And suddenly the overmastering desire to get at Harmon broke through the veneer of his caution. He swung his fist with all his force full upon Frank's mouth.

It was a powerful blow but the agent took it without flinching. He was hard, was Harmon, and used to many a rough and tumble water-front fight. Before Murray could strike again he sprang up and hit him fair on the chin. David staggered and sank down on his knees.

"There!" Gracie whispered. "You've made him say his prayers."

With a distorted face Davie got to his feet and came at Harmon again.

The next minute he lay on his back bleeding and half-stunned upon the floor. He could not rise.

"Oh, Frank," Gracie cried childishly. "You struck him very hard."

Harmon took the fine linen handkerchief from his breast pocket and wiped his damaged mouth. Gracie, her hands tightly clenched, her breast heaving, turned away her head.

"Take me home," she said in a frozen voice. "At once, please."

Chapter VI

NEXT DAY, SHORTLY after one o'clock, Daniel walked briskly down the main street of Kirkbridge. Before setting out from his home he had left a note for Kate on the kitchen table telling her that he would not be back that night—a step so reckless, so inconceivable, it was perhaps the bravest thing he had ever done in all his life.

On the way to the station he had posted a letter to Gracie reminding her to meet him the following afternoon at the houseboat.

The weather was clear and bright. As he neared the foot of the High Street of Kirkbridge Daniel, with that same intent expression, swung into the Kirkbridge Clothing Company, a large emporium, devoted to children's outfitting. Here, without hesitation, he demanded a small ready-made tweed suit, a pair of boots, woollen stockings, and a flannel shirt.

Despite his apparent hardihood, the little photographer could not repress a physical tremor as he handed over the money for his purchases. That morning, before quitting Levenford, he had withdrawn from the Savings Bank the enormous sum of £25, and ever since a vision of Kate, discovering this irreparable subtraction from their hard-won savings, had tormented him. But by an effort he mastered this weakness. With the brown paper parcel under his arm he thanked the assistant and left the shop. Presently he reached Clyde Place and vanished into the darkness of the tenement.

Ten minutes later he emerged with pale, compressed lips and a nervous flush upon his cheeks. The 20 remaining sovereigns had left his purse, and tagging along beside him, with one hand in his, the other clutching the parcel to his narrow chest, was Robert.

So deep and complex was Daniel's feeling that he simply could not speak, and they reached the tramway terminus without a word being exchanged between them. It was possible, from Kirkbridge, to reach the loch directly by tram, for the old horse coaches had recently been superseded by an electric trolley system. The journey was long and bumpy, yet Daniel had elected to take it in preference to the train, since it spared him the necessity of passing through Levenford.

Once or twice Robert glanced sideways at Daniel, but immediately he encountered Daniel's eyes he glanced away again. It was impossible to guess what his thoughts were, except that in the depths of his eyes there lurked a dark glimmer of the fear and suspicion that fought together in his breast.

Daniel could stand it no longer. He exclaimed hurriedly: "Don't be frightened."

It was about the worst thing he could have said. The boy's face shut down to a stony immobility. After an interval he muttered:

"I'm not frightened. It's just . . ." In spite of his control his mouth quivered like a puppy's. "It's just that I don't know anything about you. When I saw you that first day I didn't know you were going to take me away. If I had I wouldn't have let you up the stairs."

Daniel gave an inarticulate murmur of sympathy, and patted the small adjacent knee. But Robert was not to be cajoled. "I'm not a baby," he said. His underlip stuck out: he emphasised his words with strong, serious nods of his head. "I can fight."

They ran into Gielston, the terminus of the tramway, towards three o'clock in the afternoon. The town, clustered whitely at the foot of the loch, lay basking in brilliant sunshine, its wooden pier jutting into the clear water as though reaching out for coolness.

Daniel and Robert descended here. Hurriedly, since they had only fifteen minutes to spare, Daniel made some purchases at the Pier Provision stores. Then they took their places on the *Lomond*, a small steam ferry which left every afternoon to serve the lochside villages, and soon they were chugging across towards the opposite mountains.

And at length, higher up the winding shore, they rounded a promontory and came upon a small bay of sunbaked sand, facing due south and completely sheltered by the woods. Here, at anchor in the centre of the bay, bleached and blistered to a washed-out blue, was a queer boxed-in craft. It was Hay's houseboat. Whatever the druggist's views on the heavenly hereafter, he had chosen for his present delectation a perfect paradise on earth.

For Robert, at least, it was the final evocation. When

they reached the old warped dinghy beached on the soft sand he leaned against it and drew a long, spent breath.

"Is this the place?" he inquired in a husky voice.

Daniel nodded. "This is Cantie Bay."

A silence.

"Jesus Christ!" said Robert gravely, as though this were, indeed, the only thing to be said.

A spasm shot up Daniel's spine at the gentle blasphemy.

"Robert, you must not speak like that!"

For the moment he could say no more. Tugging on the oars, they reached the houseboat and went aboard, after tying up the dinghy. It was a battered old tub, hardly deserving to be called a pleasure boat. In its early years it had towed coal barges on the Firth and Clyde before being left to rot in harbour. Hay had found her there and looked her over with an experienced eye. After weeks of acrimonious bargaining with the owners, he had bought her, as he declared triumphantly, for the price of a poultice. He added a shaky superstructure to the hull and roughly splashed a coat of paint on the splintering timbers before having it towed to Cantie Bay. After years of sun and mud and rain the boat now blended with its surroundings and no longer looked out of place.

Leaving Robert on the bridge, Daniel went down to the galley, which consisted of little more than an iron stove, some plates and cutlery. Saucepans and an enormous frying-pan hung from nails driven into a beam. But long practice had taught Daniel to cope with worse situations than this. The pan was soon sizzling on the stove. Two eggs, skilfully cracked on the edge of the pan, were cooking in the golden fat from fried ham. In no time at all, it seemed, the tea was ready, the ham and eggs, the bread, butter and jam laid out. Daniel and Robert sat down at a table such as the boy had never before seen in his life. In his eyes surprise struggled with uncertainty. His most fixed ideas, his suspicions of Daniel and his motives, his fear of a trick, in short, his whole philosophy, learned in the hard school of his childhood, trembled on its foundations. He did not understand at all. Helped by his hunger he made a truce with himself and attacked the plentiful and savoury fare. Surely his companion could be trusted and the food would not be poisoned.

In the end he ate very little. Nothing would have pleased Daniel more than to see him devour an enormous meal. But the boy, although enticed by the quality of the food, could not manage the quantity. Halfway through his second slice of bread he put a pointed elbow on the table and gazed at Daniel.

"Can I put the rest in my pocket for tomorrow?"

"No, we will put it in the larder. It will keep better there and you can get it whenever you like."

A new look of astonishment in the serious eyes. A half slice of bread to be kept untouched, for its owner! That passed everything.

"Am I going to live here?"

"Yes. Now you are tired and must go to bed."

"To bed," repeated Robert. "I never went to bed until Auntie Lang got back from the pub at closing time. But it doesn't matter, I will go to bed if you like. But not until we have washed up."

"Don't bother about that." Daniel, trying to seem jocular, could only manage an embarrassed laugh. "I will put a big kettle of water on the stove so that you can wash."

"Wash? Me? Why? I don't need one."

"To please me."

A silence, the boy was too tired to argue. Getting up, he started to take off his rags. When Daniel brought the big bowl of steaming water he had a towel over his arm and a cake of soap in his hand. Robert started to wash. The job was not very well done. Daniel watched him while clearing the table. When the child had finished drying himself his body had the faint bluish colour of a chicken freshly plucked and trussed for market.

There were two bunks in the cabin, an upper and a lower, and Robert, given his choice, elected to be high.

"Lie down, now, there's a good boy," said Daniel.

Robert got down upon one elbow, when a final thought disturbed him. Gazing at Daniel with a strange expression he remarked: "You won't go away."

He subsided upon the bunk at last, his face turned sideways, his hair softened by its recent washing and shot with fair lights lying like flax upon the pillow. The moment he was down he was asleep.

Daniel stood motionless, looking at the sleeping child, whose regular breathing had the effect of reassuring him, of counteracting the frightful emaciation of that gaunt little face.

In repose that face lost its gutter sharpness, its worry and its watchfulness, and became completely childish and inexpressibly sad; in particular the eye shadows had a tender quality and the mouth a pitiful droop which raised in Daniel a passion of commiseration.

A great lump rose in his throat. He bit his lip hard, his head cocked sideways, his hand nervously caressing his beard. Then he turned silently and began to pick up the bits and pieces of the boy's discarded clothing.

Carefully, so as to make no sound, he wrapped them up in brown paper which had recently enclosed Robert's new suit. A round stone taken from the ballast above the bilge boards supplied the necessary weight. Carrying the package in his hand, Daniel went on deck and cast it from him into the loch. It struck the still water with barely a sound and sank immediately. Something symbolic in the action struck at Daniel and made it a fitting climax to the day. A casting away of all the child's old life: already an assumption of the new.

The dawn broke warm and fine, with a faint haze drifting over the calm surface of the loch.

Though Daniel rose early, Robert was on deck before him, fully dressed in his new clothes, and playing with an old box camera which Daniel had left on a previous visit to the boat.

Since the morning was so fine they breakfasted on deck. Halfway through a slight spasm of appreciation twisted Robert's lips—his nearest approach to a smile.

"All the same, I'm glad Annie Lang's not here."

"Why?" Daniel asked.

"Oh, you surely know. I like my clothes and she'd

pawn them. I got boots once from the Welfare Society, but she got hold of them and put them up the spout. Mind you, Annie's not a bad sort. She just had to pawn my boots."

Daniel was silent for a moment, then, seizing the opportunity, with attempted casualness he declared:

"You'll find a difference with your own mother."

Robert stopped eating. The yellow bone spoon with which he had been chasing fragments of boiled egg around the shell remained suspended, motionless, in mid-air. That spoon's immobility was more poignantly expressive than any words of the blow delivered upon his sensibilities by Daniel's remark. There had been the sunny morning, the old box camera, the adventure of breakfast upon the boat, all making him forget the ominous event hanging, hanging above his head—the advent of his mother.

He was, and had long been, minutely aware of his own circumstances, since mysteries do not survive the intimacies of Clyde Place. Before Daniel's arrival he had known that his father was dead, his mother "away", and that he himself was an illegitimate child.

It made Robert go hot and cold all over to think of this woman who laid claim to him. He would have died sooner than utter the word "mother".

"Her!" he exclaimed, and his brows drew down. "Why does she need to come? I like it here the way we are."

Daniel sighed. "I've taken a heap of trouble, boy, to bring the two of you together."

"I'm not wanting her."

"You mustn't talk that way."

Another silence.

"When is she coming?"

"This afternoon."

But at five o'clock Daniel began to manifest symptoms of restlessness. He wanted Gracie to come. He longed to unite Robert to his mother. Moreover, beyond the approaching sunset lay the harsh morning of reality. He had himself to think of and his own position, his need to be back in Levenford that night.

A physical tremor passed over him at the thought of Kate. His eyes searched the shore, his watch came out a dozen times in half as many minutes, indeed, he fidgeted nervously with the old timepiece as though it were, in part, responsible for the delay.

At last, however, he gave a sudden exclamation. "There!" he cried, pointing to the beach. "There she is at last."

The start which Robert gave belied his studied composure. He jumped nearly from his skin, and his face, coloured slightly by the day's sunshine, went pale as putty as he followed Daniel's finger towards the dark figure seen indistinctly in the distance moving through the trees.

"Into the skiff, boy," cried Daniel. "We'll get to the beach before her."

He tumbled into the dinghy, placing Robert in the bows behind him. A moment's excited sculling brought them to the verge of Cantie Bay. And then, as they turned, Daniel stiffened in his seat. The oars dropped from his hands, a cry of blank disappointment from his lips.

"It's not her," he faltered. "It's not her, after all."

Robert suddenly sat up straight, his cheeks flooding with a violent colour.

"Oh dear, oh dear," Daniel muttered to himself. "Whatever can have become of her?"

The figure striding towards them across the beach and darkening the horizon with its solemn prescience was the figure of Apothecary Hay.

Chapter VII

EARLIER THAT SAME day, in her room at College Row, Gracie was moving about in her dressing-gown, listlessly engaged in packing. Her trunk lay open on the floor, which was strewn with tissue paper, shoes, and a cardboard hatbox.

On the bed a dress stretched itself forlornly, while the drawer of the yellow chest, pulled out and empty, had a queer pathetic look, like the gaping mouth of a toothless old woman. The whole aspect of the room was indicative of change, and Gracie herself wore a depressed and fugitive air, yet her visitor, just shown up by Mrs Glen, seemed both static and unshakeable.

Stretched in the wicker chair, his hat across his eyes, surveying Gracie's movements with that heavy imperturbability which usually masked his thoughts, was Frank Harmon.

"So you're actually going?" he remarked, without moving from his chair.

She inclined her head, not looking at him, her brows maintaining their frown of troubled concentration.

"I wish you hadn't come up, Frank," she said a moment later, having folded the dress and placed it in the trunk.

"Why shouldn't I?"

"We said good-bye last night."

"Is a woman's good-bye always final?"

"It's idiotic of me, Frank, but it hurts me that you won't take me seriously. What I'm going to do isn't easy. It means a struggle for me . . . a hard struggle. But I'm going to do it."

His expression remained politely incredulous, yet he veiled his eyes to conceal the dark annoyance which rankled within him. He was, in truth, furious that Gracie should want to quit Levenford for no reason that he could understand, save that she had fallen into disrepute in the town: more furious still that, despite his best efforts and all his attentions through these past weeks, he had not, beyond a few brief, unsatisfying kisses, materially gained her favour.

He had succeeded with so many women that this unexpected failure inflamed him the more, increasing his determination to prevent her leaving him.

"Well," he said at length, "you may be right to clear out. After all, they have used you abominably here. And, actually, you're not well, Gracie. If you don't look out you'll have a breakdown. I'm worried about you."

His altered manner, kind, persuasive, eminently reasonable, brought tears to her eyes. She was, and had been since the scene last night at the Ladywell Tavern, in a highly nervous state.

"But you ought to have a real holiday," he went on, "not a makeshift affair so near this wretched town. That's why I spoke to you about Spain. It's lovely down in Malaga. Think of it. Rest, quiet, blue skies, and Mediterranean sunshine. . . ." He gazed at her intently. "I'd be good to you."

Immediately her dark pupils drew away.

"No, Frank . . . not that."

He watched her covertly, holding back his anger with an effort, considering how he might best break down her resistance.

He really wanted her, more, perhaps, than he had wanted any woman, and he was prepared to use any stratagem, to go to any lengths, to have her. With a shrug of his shoulders, as though accepting her decision, sadly, yet with a good grace, he exclaimed: "You are a wilful creature, my dear, I see you mean to have your way. Well, at least allow me to be of service to you. Let me take you and your baggage to Markinch in my car."

She gazed at him doubtfully. She was dreading the cab journey to the station under the eyes of the town, the wait at the station, the difficulty with her luggage.

"It's too much trouble for you, Frank."

"None at all. As a matter of fact I'd planned to take the day off to run down to Ardfillan—the regatta is on there this week." He stopped suddenly and his face broke into a frank smile. "Say, there's an idea. We'll both go to the regatta and I'll drive you across the hill to Markinch in the evening."

She drew herself back slightly, feeling his influence, distrusting the persuasive force of his personality. As on that previous occasion in his office, her instinct rose up suddenly, warning her against him.

"No, we couldn't do that."

"Why on earth not!" His smile widened, displaying his fine strong teeth. "It's only ten o'clock. You're so cast down, it's the very thing to cheer you up. You've always loved sailing. And a day in the open air will do you no end of good."

She had all at once a longing to be taken out of herself, to be lifted up a little before the long and arduous struggle which confronted her. Frank, yes, Frank was just the one to do it.

Then, while she still hesitated, she recollected a circumstance which might enable her to send a message to Daniel, telling him she was delayed, that she would join him later in the evening.

At that her last reluctance fell away from her.

"I'll go then, Frank." She put her hand upon his sleeve. "But be sure you get me to Markinch on time."

While Daniel rowed Hay took the tiller, sitting silent and impenetrable in the stern, an angular, black figure in a hard square hat, holding the rudder cords as though they were the strings of destiny.

Apparently he took no notice of Robert whatsoever. And certainly he took none of Daniel. His gaze was bent, with unblinking, saturnine intensity, upon a distant point of the compass. His lips, turned down, wore a slight smile of contempt. He had the air, oblivious and stoic, of an early martyr being ferried across the Styx.

Daniel, on the other hand, was in a piteous state of flutter. He dared not ask a single question, knowing his friend's irreverent tongue, for fear of startling the boy. But what he read in Hay's face did little to reassure him. Nor, when they reached the houseboat, had he the opportunity to inquire the facts, for the druggist, in a loud voice, immediately demanded tea.

He ate heartily, working his way through all that Daniel placed before him, with a thorough, metallic champing of his artificial teeth. But at last he was finished. He put down his empty cup, wiped his long dun-coloured moustache with unhurried strokes, and lay back on his seat.

"Well," he declared, as though becoming aware of Daniel for the first time, "you're not such a bad cook after all."

There was an inflection in the remark so dry, so withering, that Robert at least seemed to find it funny. He laughed, no mere spasm of tight-drawn little face, but a shrill twitter of amusement.

Hay turned slowly, recognising the boy at last. Actually no introduction would have been happier—nothing gratified the chemist more, there was no surer road to his favour, than the spontaneous appreciation of his sardonic jokes.

"So this is him," he said to Daniel after a lengthy period of inspection.

"Yes, this is Robert," Daniel answered.

"I'll say this much for him," Hay delivered the judgement with due approval, "he's not much to look at. But he seems to have a head on him."

This pronouncement, so unexpected and so flattering, had the effect of making Daniel quiver with pride. For a moment he forgot his burning anxiety to have news of Gracie.

"There isn't a lot of him . . . yet."

"Stand up, boy," said the druggist, "and let's have

a peek at you. Mmh! Ay, ay! Just as I thought! He's got the rickets."

"But something can be done about it?" Daniel said hastily. "I've been thinking it over and I fancied maybe that a leg-iron—"

"Leg-iron! Fiddle-de-dee," the druggist interrupted.

"You think they'll be able to put him right?" Daniel inquired anxiously.

"*They!*" said the druggist with an ironic laugh. "I know nothing about your 'theys'. All I know is that *I* could put him right in 12 months if I had the handling of him." He gazed hard at Robert. "Do you believe me, boy?"

"Yes," Robert muttered. "Only I'm fine the way I am."

Hay nodded his head several times with a significant air approving the sturdy independence behind the remark. Almost gleefully, he declared:

"We would get to know each other brawly if we had the chance, you and me. Away to bed now, that's a good boy. I've something to say to your friend Nimmo that'll not bear keeping."

When Robert had gone to bed, Hay turned to Daniel with a sarcastic smile.

"I like that boy. Did you notice how he hung on my words?"

"Yes, yes," said Daniel, beside himself with worry. "But tell me about Gracie. What has happened?"

"She promises she will come later, but I don't know when."

"Why, why did she not come now?"

Hay gave a little mocking smile. "Listen to me, my friend, if you are so anxious to know. At noon today, just as I was shutting the shop for lunch, your dear Gracie came running up in a great hurry to ask if I would be paying my usual visit to the boat. I told her I intended to spend an hour or two on the water. 'In that case,' she said, 'will you tell Daniel Nimmo that after going to Ardfillan I will be at the boat at seven without fail?' She thanked me and ran off before I could say a word."

Daniel relaxed.

"Seven o'clock? That will delay me, but I can still manage."

Hay looked at his friend anxiously. "You know, no doubt, that she has gone off with Frank Harmon?"

"But. . . ."

"And Harmon," Hay continued relentlessly, "has just cleared his desk for a six-week trip to Spain. He sails on the *Andalusia* from Ardfillan Pier, tonight."

Daniel swallowed dryly.

"How can you know all this?"

"I know most things that are happening in Levenford," Hay answered with a certain smugness. "Harmon's clerk was in my shop last Monday. And he told me something more."

"What?" Daniel whispered, wrung to the heart.

"When Harmon booked his passage through the agency, he took not one ticket, but two."

There was a long, frozen silence. The druggist, gazing over the top of Daniel's head, brought a sliver of liquorice from his pocket and began to chew. From time to time he smacked his lips together.

When the druggist had gone, after six o'clock, to catch the fast train from Markinch, Daniel took a seat in the stern of the boat, and in the last low gleam of colour from the western sky searched the hazy beach with straining, anxious eyes. It had turned cold, the breeze was rising, and a shiver went through him. But it could not extinguish the faith that persisted in his breast nor the hope that still flickered in his heart.

At half-past four that afternoon Harmon and Gracie had returned from the regatta to the lounge of the Ardfillan Pier Hotel.

Harmon was seated at a small table by the window with a whisky and soda before him, while Gracie, stretched on the adjoining sofa, was drinking a cup of tea.

The view was beautiful, that combination of sunlit sea and sky conducive to a gentle reverie, but the noise coming from the crowds strolling along the front made Gracie's head ache more than ever.

Her migraine had begun at lunch after Harmon had insisted on ordering champagne—which always upset her—and it had continued all afternoon when, seated with Frank in the mass of people upon the pier, surrounded by shouting, excited spectators, deafened by the brass music from the merry-go-rounds of the fair-ground behind, she had endeavoured to see, to enjoy, the regatta. What a fiasco it had been!—the very thought of it made her temples throb again.

Her eyelids fluttered with sheer nervous fatigue and yet, jaded and dejected though she was, she refused to surrender to wretchedness. She had been foolish to consent to this expedition, but it was not an irrevocable folly. She had only to endure the situation for another hour.

Meanwhile, Harmon had finished his whisky. Putting down his glass, he moved over and sat on the couch beside her, studying her with a half playful, half sardonic familiarity which set her nerves quivering anew.

"How is the head?" he inquired.

She managed to smile. "Still rather bad."

"A breath of fresh air will put you right." He spoke lightly. "I've ordered a launch for five o'clock. We'll take a trip out to the big liners."

"But Frank," she raised herself, "isn't it almost time I was going?"

"Nonsense." He dropped his big hand on her knee with an easy intimacy. "I want to show you the *Andalusia.* She's a lovely boat. We fitted her out, you know. The staterooms are the last word."

There was a pause. A strange thought flickered to the surface of her mind. She glanced away, her nervousness increased.

"I know you mean to be kind, Frank, but I'm not really in the mood for a ship inspection."

He laughed. "You may change your mind when you're on board."

Shocked out of her lassitude, she lowered her eyes, striving to keep a firm grip of herself. What had at first seemed a wild suspicion now assumed an aspect of probability which sent a cold shiver through her veins. Had she not heard somewhere that the *Andalusia* was listed for an imminent departure?

A fresh surge of anxiety and indignation swept over her. Only by a great effort did she restrain an impulse to question him directly and settle the issue at once. But a scene would gain her nothing. She had a worrying idea that he was watching her, waiting for her next move, prepared calmly to counter it.

There and then, stifled by the sensation of his proximity, she experienced an overmastering, an almost terrifying desire to escape from him. She would have given everything she possessed to be miles and miles away, never to see him again, never, never. But now, above all, she must disguise her feelings. She forced a smile, made a gesture of acquiescence.

"Oh, very well, Frank. If you're set on it, we'll go."

"Good."

She sat up, glanced at her watch.

"I'll go and tidy up. I must put some cologne on my forehead."

His expression changed slightly, and he gave her a narrow, slanting glance. He said slowly: "Don't be long."

"I shan't keep you a minute."

She crossed the lounge and went into the rest-room, where she stood perfectly motionless, thinking deeply, with a pale and drawn brow. She felt limp, as though floating in an enervating air.

But in a few moments she saw exactly what she must do. A train left Ardfillan for Renton at half-past five—

the very rarity of the service had impressed it on her memory. From Renton she would walk to Markinch—it was a longish way, but in her present apprehension she counted that as nothing. And then—a faint expression of relief softened her harassed features—she would reach Daniel and the boy.

If only she could have stolen away unnoticed without further delay! But that, in the circumstances, was impossible. She must use her wits, rely upon some simple stratagem. Cautiously, she opened the door. As she had expected, Harmon was in the lobby, awaiting her. She summoned her brightest smile, advanced towards him and took his arm.

"Now I feel better. The lounge was rather stuffy."

They passed through the lobby to the front porch of the hotel. Suddenly, with a start of recollection, and by an effort keeping her voice natural, Gracie exclaimed:

"Oh, how stupid. I left my bag on the sofa: will you get it for me, Frank?"

There was the barest pause, almost imperceptible, during which she held herself rigid, her smile fixed resolutely, as though painted upon her lips. She had guessed that he could not, without absolute discourtesy, refuse so simple a request.

"All right," he said slowly, turning on his heel. "Wait here till I come back."

Her heart began to beat again. For an instant she forced herself to be still, but no sooner had he disappeared behind the brass-bound revolving door than she stepped quickly into the street. Her purse was in her pocket. For the time being she had abandoned completely all thought of her luggage. She wanted only to get away, to get away while this opportunity remained.

Outside, she simply flew to the station, took her ticket hurriedly and flung herself into a front compartment of the train, which, since Ardfillan was the terminus of the line, stood waiting at the outbound platform.

Not daring to show herself at the window she sat back, scarcely breathing during what seemed an interminable delay. But at last the whistle sounded and the train jerked slowly away. She sighed with relief.

It was nearly eight o'clock when they finally drew into Renton, and Gracie, stepping on to the platform, felt a surge of energy in her limbs. The evening was still and silent, and the thought of the long walk ahead was not displeasing to her.

It was after ten o'clock when she reached the bay. She felt the dry softness of the sand beneath her feet. She was at the water's edge now, halted, her eyes searching, her breath quickened by expectation. Ah yes, there was the light of the binnacle lantern. Then dimly in the darkness the glimmer of the houseboat took form, lying out there in the inky shallows.

Cupping her hands about her mouth she called out: "Cooee! Daniel! Daniel!"

Immediately there came an answer in tones of joyful recognition.

"Gracie, is that you?"

"Yes," she cried, all her being suffused by happiness and relief. As she heard Daniel row towards her in the dinghy she felt that she had reached a safe haven at last.

The next day came fresh and fair. It had rained heavily during the night, but in the morning, although the wind remained high, the sun broke through the racing clouds and steeped the loch in brightness. To Gracie, seated on the deck of the houseboat with her son, the world wore a strange new aspect.

They were alone. After breakfast Daniel had departed hurriedly for Levenford.

And now, sheltered by the high bulwarks, over which the crested "white horses" of the loch were visible, Gracie and Robert were playing a game of draughts.

Gazing at his small intent face, the dark eyes downcast towards the board, the long lashes casting shadows upon the pale, still hollow cheeks, the lips compressed in contemplation of his next move, there welled up in Gracie such an emotion of longing, mingled with remorse, it seemed as though her heart must break. Why, but for Daniel and the intervention of a forgiving heaven, had she almost thrown away the most precious thing which life could give?

All that she had dreaded had not even remotely come to pass. Her meeting with her child had taken place simply, without one of those agonising embarrassments which she had feared might arise to shame her.

He had accepted her, neither eagerly nor fondly, yet without a word of recrimination: had heard in unreproachful silence her halting explanation, that laboured story of her protracted stay in India: had behaved throughout with a quiet sense of knowing everything, of holding nothing against her, merely of leaving the whole solution of the problem to the future.

And how quickly, she reflected joyfully, how quickly their mutual adjustment was taking place. The instincts of nature were not to be denied. Already his stoic reticence was breaking down, with guarded, reluctant, half-hidden glances he was drawing towards her, and once, by some well-chosen word, she had evoked from him a shy, appreciative smile.

Moist-eyed, she pledged herself to care for her forgotten little boy with the most tender, the most constant solicitude. She perceived, as by a lightning flash, how frivolous, how self-centred had been her life, realised also how, in future, she might find happiness, in giving her most devoted service to the child.

The future opened up like the clear, fresh pages of a book in which the record of her accomplishment would be inscribed. With Daniel's help she would find honest employment, she would try so hard, so earnestly, work her fingers to the bone, to make a good and worthy home.

The time passed all too quickly, and she saw, with a throb of joy, how groundless had been her fear that her company would intimidate or bore Robert. When evening came it was hard to get him below. But at last the darkness forced them down, and in the galley he helped her to cook supper of fried ham and scrambled eggs.

Often, with the coming of the evening, a sort of listless melancholy would fall on Gracie, but now she was gay, gayer than she had been for many months, with a gaiety so infectious that it melted even the gravity which the sadness of his life had imposed on Robert. He laughed and chattered, unguarded, unselfconscious, carried away by the flowing tide of happiness which bore them both along.

When he climbed into his bunk—wisely, she resisted her inclination to assist him—she bethought herself to sing to him. And, listening to an old Scots lullaby, he fell asleep.

When she had washed the dishes, thinking that her movements in the narrow cabin might awake him, she went on deck. The wind seemingly had dropped and, mindful of her new responsibility as cook and caterer, she decided she must go to the Ross farm to obtain fresh supplies of eggs, butter and fresh milk. This would take her little more than ten minutes. The farm lay conveniently, barely a half-mile back in the woods, and Apothecary Hay bought most of his stores from its good-natured owner.

Quietly, then, Gracie untied the dinghy from its mooring at the stern of the houseboat and rowed the few yards to the shore. There she beached the little skiff and started across the meadows towards the trees.

It was dark, gustier than she had expected, and the pines made a heavy sighing as she went through the wood. Soon, however, she was at the farm, and having made her purchase and chatted a moment with the farmer's wife, she set off briskly on the return journey.

Suddenly at the end of the wood, as she crossed the deserted country road which wound its way along the margin of the loch, she saw the lights of a slow, approaching vehicle.

At first she took it for a belated farm wagon lumbering back to its lonely steading, then she realised that it was a car, and drew back instinctively to let it pass.

But when the beam of the yellow headlamps picked out her stationary figure a thought struck into her which sent a cold thrill through her breast. Prompted by this sudden and instinctive apprehension, even as the car slowed down and stopped she hurried forward across the road and began rapidly to make her way towards the beach.

But she had been seen—someone called from behind her. That call, more than anything, increased her fear, set her running across the meadow with a wildly beating heart. Burdened as she was, and unfamiliar with the path, she stumbled on the tufty hummocks of the field, blundered into bushes and thick undergrowth. Twice she fell to her knees.

She was afraid now, horribly afraid, and the sound of someone following increased her panic. Someone was close behind her. Her feet were bogged in the soft sand of the beach. With a sobbing breath she spun round, her figure braced, feeling for an agonising instant that she must faint. She made to cry out, but no sound left her dry throat. Yes, she had known it. The man who stood before her was Harmon.

She stood there, too overcome to speak, too petrified to move. His physical nearness to her, utterly unexpected, intensified by the darkness and the solitude, was more than she could humanly sustain. He must have read the shrinking in her face, for, still breathing thickly, he took her by the arm.

"Yes . . . you deserve a thorough shaking . . . you've led me a pretty dance."

"I'm sorry, Frank," she faltered palely. It was all she could find to say.

"I should hope you are." He had recovered his breath now, and there was in his tone a measured note of reason, a sort of husky firmness more ominous than anger. "You didn't really imagine I'd let you get away from me. I'm not the sort of man you can play hot and cold with, Gracie."

She lowered her eyes, struggling for composure, while thoughts raced madly in her anguished brain. What, oh what, a senseless fool she had been ever to have had a thing to do with Frank, to have accepted his favours, flirted with him, and above all to have so misjudged him as to believe he would tamely accept the dismissal she had attempted to impose upon him.

"I wasn't taken in," he went on in that same even tone. "I suspected at Ardfillan you were up to some trick. But I thought you might have played a better one. It was easy for me to follow you. But if you wanted a holiday you might have chosen a livelier place than this. It's all so stupid, Gracie. And against your own interests. Anyhow, you're coming with me in the car right away."

"No, Frank, no." she whispered.

"It's no use to argue," he answered flatly. "Things have gone too far between us. We've missed the *Andalusia* up here, but we can join her at Tilbury."

Her blood congealed. For a second she had a frantic impulse to scream for help, but a glimmer of reason told her how useless that would be—her voice would never carry from this lonely spot. Besides, she might wake Robert, and this above all was what she dreaded most. Come what may, Harmon and Robert must be kept apart. If ever she saw a gleam of understanding of her situation in that childish eye, then, simply, she would die. She felt all at once weak and vulnerable. The hard brilliance with which she might once have withstood Harmon was gone for ever, lost in the tender softness of her new protective love for her son.

Yet this instinct gave her resources of another kind—her mind, never more lucid, went on working with a desperate, distracted energy, seeking a way of escape. And suddenly, in a flash of revelation, she saw what she could do.

"Frank," she murmured at last. "If I do come, will you promise to be nice to me?"

"Didn't I say so?" His face cleared slightly.

"Very well," she said submissively. "I'll go and tell Daniel."

At first he did not understand, then, following her eyes, he saw the feeble light on the boat.

"Old Nimmo is with you?"

"Yes," she lied, "I can't leave without a word."

"I'll come aboard and have a word with him."

"No, Frank," she said firmly. "I must take him the provisions, then I will make some sort of excuse, get my hat, and join you."

He kept an angry silence.

"Don't you understand? You have got your way,"

she cried bitterly. "Are you afraid I shall escape? How could I do that?"

Then, more calmly, "Smoke a cigarette. I will be back before you have finished it."

"Very well. But if you are not back in five minutes I shall come and get you."

"That won't be necessary," she said.

Suppressing the wild beating of her heart, she put her parcel in the dinghy and, with an air of resignation, took the oars. Drawing away from the shore, she saw the flame from a match as Harmon lit his cigarette. Knowing he could no longer see her, she bent over the oars. Her plan was quite clear in her mind. Frank was blocking the bay of Cantie so that she could not escape that way. But he had forgotten, or perhaps, as a stranger to the district, he did not know that beyond the headland, on the opposite shore of the loch, stood the little port of Gielston. She could easily reach it. It was little more than two miles and Gracie, resolute, felt that she could cover five times that distance. She would take Robert, book a room in an hotel and telephone Daniel and, if necessary, warn the police. There must be no more half-measures and futile attempts at escape; once and for all she must remove this threat and be sure of her freedom.

With a quick stroke of the oars she had brought the dinghy alongside the houseboat and climbed on to the bridge. Her legs were trembling so much that she had difficulty in holding herself erect. In the cabin she put out her hand and gently shook Robert's shoulder.

He opened his big eyes.

"Robert," she said, trying to smile, "we are going on a little trip. Now. . . ."

The child looked at her in astonishment.

"Where are we going?"

"To Gielston . . . and after that to Uncle Daniel's house. It is much better than this place."

Gracie had expected a protest, some sign of alarm, or at least of petulance at this unexpected derangement of his rest. But all his life Robert had been subject to upsets and turmoil, to the sudden descent upon him of the unforeseen.

Moreover, because of their happy day together, he trusted her. He rose without fuss, and while the flame of the candle threw his little shadow in fantastic shapes upon the bulkhead began philosophically to dress.

An instant later they were in the dinghy, he in the stern, a blanket across his knees, she in the thwarts with her arms taut against the oars. Scarcely breathing, she dipped the blades in silence and, using the cover of the houseboat, slid away into the darkness of the night.

As she did so, a few heavy drops of rain began to fall, splashing upon the water, as though the invisible sky were dripping tears. But although she was bareheaded and without a coat, she did not mind the wet. Suffused by a trembling exaltation she could think of nothing but the mercy of their escape. For a moment the tiny pinpoint of Harmon's cigarette showed faintly on the shore, then she rounded the promontory and it vanished from her sight.

In the bay it had been easy to propel the skiff, but now she was beyond the point, and had started to cross the loch, the going became more difficult. There were no large waves, at least, none was visible to her in the blackness, yet she felt a choppy tide against her and the boat bounced and veered occasionally, in an awkward manner. She put her shoulders into the work, however, and made steady advance towards the opposite shore.

About halfway over the skiff took a sharp dip, reared its bow high into the air, then smacked down hard upon the water. At the same moment Gracie's cheek was stung by a strong gust of wind and a harder spatter of the driving rain.

She had known the loch since her childhood and was quick to realise that they had quitted the shelter of Inchlade Island, which lay about a mile farther to the north, and were now in open, unprotected water. But although prepared for some worsening of weather she had not expected the wind and waves to hit them with such severity. The dinghy was in fact plunging and pitching in a disturbing manner, less from heavy seas than from a rolling ground swell, the aftermath of storm.

And suddenly Gracie became aware of herself, alone with Robert in the darkness, upon this heaving waste of waters, far from the shore and the islands, and the shapeless mountains beyond. All that she had heard of the treachery of this loch, the unplumbed depths and dangerous currents, the sudden gusts and squalls that struck without warning from the clefted hills, fell upon her with cold and terrifying force. Had she been wise to take this course, or was it her worst, her all-surpassing and most reckless folly?

Twisting round on the rocking thwarts she glanced towards the opposite shore and was reassured by the lights of Gielston, perhaps not more than three-quarters of a mile away. This, then, was still her best objective, and with a fresh access of determination she drove the tossing skiff towards it.

Holding tightly to the gunwale, Robert, during all this time, had not uttered a single word. His gaze remained fixed on his mother's face and, although stiff with uncertainty, was on the whole steady and unafraid. Meeting those trusting eyes, Gracie was overwhelmed by a new upsurge of feeling.

"It's all right, Robert," she reassured him, between her gasping breaths. "Only a little rough . . . we'll soon be there."

Alas, despite her efforts, the lights of the friendly town crept nearer with agonising slowness. Her spine was breaking, her breast constricted, her raw and blistered hands gave her excruciating pain. The wind, ever growing, sapped her strength and fought her like a live thing, throwing her back, it seemed, with every yard she gained.

Now the high swell was topped by spanning crests, which broke over the bows and drenched the tiny craft. The flying spray had soaked her to the skin, plastered her hair against her dripping face. She wanted to weep, to give up, sink into oblivion. Yet she kept on, urging the boat forward by the sheerest effort of her will.

Then, as she pulled blindly, her strength almost

spent, the skiff lifted dizzily, she missed the water with one oar, which, meeting no resistance, spun from the rowlock, and as she fell backwards vanished into the surrounding void.

A stab of mortal horror pierced her. Now indeed they were lost. She raised herself slowly, grasping the sides of the wildly gyrating boat. The lights of Gielston were near, the lantern of the pier not more than a quarter of a mile away but still, in this gale, far beyond the reach of any human voice. She shivered.

"Robert," she said to him, "come to me."

He had seen the oar go over, had read her face, and was crying quietly, crying into himself, it seemed, the tears coursing silently down his cheeks. But he obeyed and crawled on his hands and knees to the centre thwart. Now there was nothing she could do but hold him closely in her arms in the bottom of the boat, shielding him as best she could, feeling the rapid patter of his heart against her breast, murmuring in his ear tender, inarticulate words. And all the time praying in her heart:

"Oh God, anything, anything but that . . . he is so helpless and so small."

The skiff was now completely out of control, yet by a freak of chance, or perhaps by reason of some inshore current, as though to mock all Gracie's agonised and useless striving, it drifted, sluggishly at first, then with increasing speed, towards the Gielston pier. As she peered across the misted water a feverish hope caught Gracie by the throat, rushed through her chilled veins like fire.

"Robert," she cried, "I believe we'll do it." And, raising her voice as the distance narrowed, she shouted with all her power. There was no answer.

The little boat, deeper than ever in the water, seemed likely to founder at any moment. Rigidly, she crouched, while the rain poured down upon her, running into her eyes, blinding her, and again she shouted out loud. Then, to her joy, her delirious joy, there came an answering shout, and dimly she saw figures running on the pier.

At that instant the dinghy, sweeping violently towards the pier, struck the big iron buoy which marked the entrance to the harbour and which, in the swirling darkness, had been quite invisible to Gracie. The force of the impact was tremendous. There was a sickening crash. The light craft spun like a teetotum, broke its back, and fell asunder. As Gracie cried, a high despairing cry, she and the boy were pitched into the black loch.

The shock was devasting. When she hit the water her grip loosened, and on coming to the surface she saw Robert drifting away from her. Her whole thought was for the child. Immediately she struck out, seized him, and struggled back to the buoy.

Desperately, sustaining Robert with one arm, fighting the swirl and race of water, she tried to get a finger-hold upon the iron sides. But the sides, though rusted, were round and rimless, and the heavy mass, oscillating giddily upon its mooring chain, crashed at one instant dangerously towards her, and the next swayed out beyond her reach.

She perceived, however, her eyes straining upwards, that the top was perfectly flat with a heavy ring welded into the centre of its ample surface. At that, she knew what she must do. Oh, God, she prayed again, let me succeed in this one thing.

Supporting the child beneath his armpits with both her hands, she somehow managed to keep afloat and waited, her pale lips drawn back, waiting till the buoy swung down to the lowest point of its arc. Then, with all her might, she strove to raise him to the level surface. She failed. Again she tried and again the crashing thing eluded her, tearing the skin from both her forearms as it bobbed and swung away.

Her strength was gone, the weight of her skirt was dragging her down. Desperately, unmindful of her own safety, she came closer and this time, somehow, she forced him up to the flat top and to safety. A great triumphant sob broke from her. There, for the fraction of a second, with upturned face, she saw him clinging to the ring, then before she could get back the huge weight of iron plunged down and smashed upon her forehead.

The sound of the impact was lost in the night, but out of the darkness a flash of brightness seared into Gracie's brain. For one swift second she knew that now, indeed, she was upon the threshold of her ending. Then the roar of the wind and the hissing of the rain, the icy chill of the water which enclosed her, all melted from her consciousness.

Her upturned brow, pale speck upon the immense blackness of the loch, was directed towards the sky, where before her glazing vision a great dull redness seemed to break and burn. Sparks flashed in that heavenly glow like the golden corolla of a bursting flower in which she saw, still, the face of Robert. Then, even as the rescue boat drew near, the waters closed above her head.

Chapter VIII

ONE EVENING IN the following spring Apothecary Hay, having shut up his shop, took his customary stroll towards the toll road.

As he neared the house of Daniel Nimmo his pace insensibly increased, and his air, as he stood at the front door rapping its glass panel with his bony knuckles, was both eager and impatient.

Kate let him in herself. He passed into the parlour, where, at a table by the open window, Daniel sat engrossed with Robert behind a heap of books. With every appearance of conforming to custom the druggist sank in silence into a third chair and stretched his long shanks beneath the table.

"Well!" Hay exclaimed, assuming a tone of patronage. "What are we up to tonight?"

Daniel raised his head, as though becoming aware of his old friend for the first time. His manner was reflective, mildly impatient.

"It may interest you to know that we've mastered the decimal system. Before you came in we had a try at a difficult sum—and, believe me, he got it right."

"Yes?" Though the exclamation was pointedly noncommittal, Hay's gaze travelled instinctively towards the scholar. Reddening slightly, Robert smiled at him, not the old wry contortion of his face but a genuine boyish smile.

It was not merely the smile, the change in him had to be seen to be believed. The lack-lustre eye was gone, and the sallow parchment skin; there was flesh on his bones and a firmness in his cheeks. His brow no longer seemed translucent, and his head was planted securely on his shoulders without threatening, from sheer debility, to topple sideways.

Nor was the alteration solely physical. Something had dropped away from Robert, that shell of precocity, revealing beneath a serious, a sensitive intelligence. The acme surely was achieved by that flush at Daniel's praise—Robert was beginning to be shy!

"In point of fact," Daniel remarked with an assumption of casualness, "I've seldom known a boy so quick to learn."

"Don't give the boy brain fever."

"God bless my soul, what do you take me for? It takes me all my time to hold him back. He likes learning."

The argument was interrupted by the entry of Kate with a tray, which she slid along the table among the books with a feminine disregard of all the places which Daniel had carefully marked in them.

"Here's the young man's supper," she declared, pouring a tumbler of fresh milk from the jug. "And since there were new pancakes going, I fetched some in for the rest of you. Don't you think Robert is getting a fine, big boy, Mr Hay?"

"Mmh!" said the druggist, with his mouth full.

"Doctor Todd was saying only yesterday that his legs have improved wonderful."

"Todd!" said Hay in a pitying voice, reaching out for another pancake. "What does he know about it? The man's in his dotage."

"Tut, tut, Mr Hay."

"Here, boy," the druggist commanded. "Stand up and let me have a look at you."

Obediently, Robert stood up, while Hay, first leaning back in his chair for the long-distance view, then leaning forward and running his fingers over the boy's shins, made an examination impressively expert. No specialist from London or Paris could have shown more aplomb or suggested more profound and intimidating knowledge. Finally he lay back in his chair, tapping his teeth with his thumbnail.

"*He'll do!*" he declared in a voice of complete omniscience. "There's calcium in his bones now." He glanced pointedly at Daniel. "I think I told you once before, on a certain occasion, that he *would* do. And I repeat—*he will do!*" Suddenly, his profundity dissolved, and he broke into his rare, neighing laugh, like a cab-horse having hysterics. "I tell you, Dan'l Nimmo, one day his legs'll be straighter nor yours. I've always said you were bow-leggit."

"Tut, tut," Kate interposed again, not over-pleased. "That's no way to talk, Mr Hay. And before the boy, too." She passed her arm about Robert's shoulders. "He is getting tall, though. Upon my word, he's nearly up to my shoulder."

"Yes," agreed Hay in a measured tone. "He's at the

growing age. He ought to have been in bed half an hour since."

"And he would too, only he wanted to wait up to see you." Kate smiled, belying the tartness of her retort, and took Robert by the arm. "Come away now, say good-night or Mr Hay'll be prescribing castor oil for all of us."

When they had gone and the two men were left alone, a silence fell. Hay, silently stroking his moustache, kept darting glances at Daniel in his most cantankerous style, as though inviting him to start an argument. But Daniel, sitting with his fingertips pressed together and a rapt, a listening expression on his face, was too absorbed to pay much attention to his friend. And so at last Hay was forced to say, in his most provoking tone: "You're looking mighty pleased with yourself."

"Ah-ah!" Daniel answered, not hearing a word.

"It's not to be wondered at, of course," went on the druggist, biting his lip as though testing his own gall. "With all the town running after you and crowding to be photographed at the studio by the plaster saint of Levenford. There's nobody comes for paregoric to my shop just to see if I've sprouted wings. No, no! But it's different with yourself, naturally. You deserve it!"

Unmindful of the satire, Daniel answered quietly: "People in this town aren't so bad, Apothecary. They feel they've behaved unjustly. And they're trying to make up for it."

Hay darted a strange glance at Daniel.

"That won't bring Gracie back."

"No," Daniel sighed, his face turning sad. "And yet

. . . recently I've had the strangest feeling. It was tragic, poor Gracie's death . . . but she died at her very best, and that's something for which we must thank God. She was a strange girl, Hay. . . . She felt too deeply and let herself be too easily influenced. At the end, she was the victim of her own emotions. I loved her more than anyone and yet I often ask myself if she would have been able to live the sort of life I was arranging for her. She would have left for one reason or another, breaking more than one heart. As it is, she has left us with a memory of which we can be proud—which will always be dear to us."

The druggist considered this epitaph in silence.

"Have you any news of Frank Harmon?" he said at last.

"No," answered Daniel, shaking his head. "He is always in the East. I don't think he will ever come back to Levenford."

"David Murray is doing well," said Hay, who seemed determined to extract a full confession.

Daniel smiled gently.

"Yes, David is settling down with Isabel. He will make a good husband . . . and a good father. He is not made for adventure. All things considered, it has turned out well."

A sound from the next room interrupted him.

In the kitchen—wonder of wonders!—Kate was singing.

"You see," said Daniel.

"Yes, yes," said the druggist, testily. "The ways of the Lord are mysterious and we are nothing but simpletons. Wait until the boy grows up and you will see how he turns out!"

"I am not worried about that, and neither are you," Daniel answered simply. "You love him as much as I do."

Getting out of his chair he laid his hand on the druggist's shoulder. "What's the use of arguing, my friend? It is a fine night and I have picked a bunch of early snowdrops to take to the cemetery."

He stood in silence for a moment. In his dreaming eyes was a tenderness, a memory, and a regret for things that were no more.

"If you have the time we could go together and put them on Gracie's grave."

The moon was shining steadily, brilliantly, above the firs, as the two friends walked slowly, side by side, towards the field of rest.